Alexander Hay Japp

Dramatic Pictures, English Rispetti, Sonnets and Other Verses

Alexander Hay Japp

Dramatic Pictures, English Rispetti, Sonnets and Other Verses

ISBN/EAN: 9783337376697

Printed in Europe, USA, Canada, Australia, Japan

Cover: Foto ©Andreas Hilbeck / pixelio.de

More available books at **www.hansebooks.com**

ENGLISH RISPETTI

SONNETS AND OTHER VERSES

BY

ALEXANDER H. JAPP

LL.D. F.R.S.E.

AUTHOR OF

'THOREAU: A STUDY,' 'ANIMAL ANECDOTES,' 'THE CIRCLE OF THE YEAR,' ETC.

London

CHATTO & WINDUS, PICCADILLY

1894

' If winter winds wail wildly round,
What better can we do,
Than seek the shelter I have found
So often, Friends, with you?'

CONTENTS

I. DRAMATIC PICTURES.

II. ENGLISH RISPETTI.

III. NARRATIVE AND LYRICAL.

IV. SONNETS.

V. TRANSLATIONS.

I. DRAMATIC PICTURES.

I. NEW LAY OF A SOLDIER BOLD.

(THE TALE OF AN ESSEX-SUFFOLK BOY'S EXPERIENCES IN
THE WEST INDIES AND AFGHANISTAN.)

WHEN first I thought o' listin' I moind the sergeant said,
'To don the red coat is the way to fetch the British maid :'
By George ! I've found it downroight true, in every place I've
    been—
In Indiar and in Burmar, an' Jamaicar, fur the Queen.

Where yeller fever waits for you, an' snappin' werry woide,
What would the British soldier do wi' no gal by his soide
To cheer he, an' a Creel* may be a warm an' tidy bit,
An' a fair Mullater I knew onct was a charmin' gal and fit.

A roight-down 'appy gal was she, and purty, too, I'm dem !
An' I on'y wish I 'ad her 'ere, to show longsoide o' them
As often thinks theirselves so 'igh, and thinks a soldier low—
Aside my gay Mullater gal they'd look uncommon slow !

She fetched I, I can tell 'ee ; an' onct I tried a song,
To let my mates know 'ow I fared† when on my walks so long.
A purty song, they said it was—I 'most forget it now—
But Dick O'Dowd went jawring‡ so as got me in a row !

    * Creole, of course, he means.   † Fared—felt.
    ‡ Jawing, no notion of 'jarring.'

He say a darkie's werry well to walk wi' i' the dark,
But a gal as shows no loight by day can scace be called a
    spark ;
A bit o' colour nice, o' course, for them as cudn' be
Longside the whoites, as was so scace, which roused the
    black in me !

Says I, 'My friend, you're "Oirish," an' can't get no gal to go
Wi' you at all, because your face is, loike your tongue,
    a blow ;'
At this he jumps upon I, loike a cat fur mouse as springs ;
But he foinds the boy was ready, an' round his breast I brings

My arms so toight, I squeezes he till his face was red as red,
An' then on floor I dashes he, wi' a smart crack on 'is 'ead ;
An' our mates they cums an' parts us then, declarin' there
    'oud be
Some mischief done as would disgrace the regiment well
    as me.

You'd loike to 'ear the song, you say, for the gay Mullater
    gal ?—
Well, wait a bit ; I'll troy the rhoymes roight back agen to
    call :
Yes, now I 'ave it—listen : 'tis as true as death, I say—
It's the song I made to cheer me when I left her far fro'
    gay :

MY GAY MULLATER GAL.

I meets 'er walkin' on the way
By sugar-canes at close o' day,
    As down the sun do fall
All of a 'eap, as ye moight say,
Wi' railway speed to stop the day,
An' bring the welcome noight fur play—
    My gay Mullater gal !

My gay Mullater gal, I say,
I meets 'er walkin' on the way,
    By sugar-canes so tall :
Says I, ' My purty maid, yer know
The British soldier's ways, an' so
You will wi' me a-walkin' go,
    My gay Mullater gal !

'You will wi' me a-walkin' go ?'
She say, ' The soldier's stoyle I know ;
    But that is not quoite all—
You give me promise to be true,
An' then I shall walk out wi' you ;
An' me you'll find a staunch true-blue '—
    My gay Mullater gal !

I gave the promise she 'ad sought,
An' straight my lips to hers I brought,
    An' on 'er neck did fall :
She say, ' Oh fie ! to promise *so*,
When you should loud, protestin', go,
Wi 'and on 'igh, an' swear, By Jo' !'
    My gay Mullater gal !

An' then she looks on I, roight sweet,
An' says I must kneel at 'er feet,
    Because I looked so tall,
That she moight jes' for once look o'er
A soldier's 'ead, as promise bore
O' constancy, an' so much more—
    My gay Mullater gal !

We walked till shadders dark fell down,
An' then came back into the town—
    But that—that wasn't all !—

We frequent met an' did the same,
An' surely me you wouldn' blame
For lookin' arter such fine game—
　　　My gay Mullater gal!

An', ah! 'ow oft I wonder now
Jes' 'ow she is, an' if 'er vow
　　　To me she's kep' thro' all:
She swore she ever would refrain
Fro' walkin' wi' the soldiers vain
But wait till I cum báck again,
　　　My gay Mullater gal!

The women wait while soldiers march!
Heigho! they often lose their starch,
　　　An' sadly go thro' all;
The soldier falls in siege or foight,
Or, wounded, ne'er agen gets roight,
His sweet'art poines in mournful ploight—
　　　Oh, poor Mullater gal!

Oh, poor Mullater girl! what's worse?
Your soldier meets new gals, o' course,
　　　Where he has gone, an' all
He acts wi' them as onct wi' you,
An' though he foinds they a'n't true-blue,
He thinks it gay, an' broight an' new!
　　　Oh, poor Mullater gal!

Well, that's the song. I 'ope, now, as you loikes it as well as
　　　they
As 'eard it when I made it fur to keep me broight an' gay;
But now I scace can sing it fur the fear o' breakin' down,
For I 'eard the poor Mullater gal lies buried in the town!

Well, well, 'tis plain we all must doy, an' grievin' a'n't no
   good,
But a feller can't but feel such toimes, he a'n't quite made
   o' wood ;
They call us soldiers rough an' that—I knows a many men
As tender i' their 'earts as gals, but 'on't quoite say it plain.

What was it made 'em foight indeed loike lions jes' set free,
At Lucknow, an' at Delhi, an' at Cawnpore and Roorkee?
But the tender 'earts all yearnin' fur the women an' the kids
In danger, an' went joyously to death as duty bids?

They say of Tommy Atkins, as he's good cause fur to blame:
By George ! 'tis true, o' stoppages an' wittles all the same ;
An' 'is grog ain't allus jes' ezactly what it oughter be,
An' there's a bloomin' swindle in supplies o' toggery.

He'd need to 'ave the pick o' gals in far lands, as at 'ome—
'Tis summat set agin the way they makes 'im starve an'
   roam :
Ye can't expec' as rollin' stones should gather much o' moss,
'Tis summat if the pick o' gals can save 'im growin' cross.

Ye cum arf-starve 'im of his grub from four o' arternoon,
'Till early morn nex' day—'tis 'ard !—you'd hear another
   tune,
If Tommy didn' cum for treat fro' gals in many lands,
An' demme, if it doesn't seem the thing to reason stands.

You can't expec' jes' much o' *go* fro' hungry men, I'm
   blowed—
An empty stomach never yet the foighten-loine well toed ;
An' onct I 'eard a Scottie say, as Burns's foinest loine
Was ' clap in 's cheek a Hoighland gill,' which, to my mind,
   is foine.

If also you ha' loined 'im well wi' beef an' greens an' duff—
A feller as ain't much hisself may then do work that's rough;
But let young swells o' officers jes' troy the lack o' fare
From four p.m. till on 'em blows nex' mornin's keener air !

Three ha'pence for yer breakfast !   Yes, jes' think on it, an'
        troy
'Ow much of a variety the bloomin' lot will buoy.
Whoy, yer can't scace get a hegg for that, a 'soldier,' * or a
        ' scrape,'†
Enough to let yer feel it when the hunger makes ye gape !

I've 'eard as good Sir Evelyn, wi' Burnett boy his soide,
Has made a change as keeps the bones and stock-pots boilin'
        woide ;
An' gets for Tommy Atkins many tid-bits—extra fare,
As war nought but wasted, or they went for other fellers'
        share.

Well, that will do, though still it is but promise of to cum ;
Poor Tommy needn' yet go about a-beaten' o' the drum ;
There's a deal to mend in other ways to set the soldier free
O' charges, an' them stoppages an' bits o' toggerie !

But what you wants to know, you say, is about Afghanistan :
Well, of all the parts I iver knew, it is the rummiest one—
A country all of rocks and hills, with scace a shade o' tree—
Well, I went there for dooty, an' it ain't the place for me.

All out about Cabul it lays roight risky i' the sun—
It ain't out there the soldier thinks o' 'avin' any fun ;

* Red-herring, so-called from his red coat ; like to like ; the
soldiers are fond of ' soldiers.'—ED.
    † Butter thinly spread upon bread.

An' when ye're out at noighttime, don't the bats go whiskin'
  boy,
An' brush yer cheeks, an' fellers, too, as big as they can floy.

Ye speaks o' owls an' 'awks, an' that; they're nought to
  Cabul bats—
Big brutes wi' wings loike eagles', an' mouths jes' loike to
  rats';
I tellee 'tis a foine su'proise the fust o' them to see,
As they drop upon ye as ye sleep below ' the greenwood
  tree ' !

You doubts it !—Well, then, cum along an' see the ones I
  shot—
Although they ain't ezackly of the kind to *go to pot*—
Look here ! you 'ave 'em large as life, an' beauties, I'll be
  bound !
A little durty now, yer see, through travellin' o'er the
  ground.

I brings 'em jes' to show my friends what loikes are Cabul
  bats—
Their woide wings stretch loike eagles'—see ! their mouths
  jes' like to rats'—
Oh, a foine su'proise it is, indeed, the fust o' them ter see;
An' oft I've shocked the ladies by a showin' 'em sudden*ly*.

Good Lord ! I moinds when I cums 'ome, I puts Bell in
  a fit—
That's Cousin Bell, yer know, as set jes' where you now do
  sit—
She'd arf a fancy for I—fact !—but took it orf entoire,
When I puts my big bat on 'er neck, an' she noigh jumps
  i' the foire.

If I 'adn't cotched her quick, yer see, 'twould been all hup
      wi' she—
For she fainted orf, an' screamed an' fell roight forrard sud-
      den*ly*—
An' 'twas a job to get 'er round, an' then, wi'out a word,
Roight orf she goes, an' never comes to see I nor the bird !

Poor Bell ! yer know we 'ad a bit o' boy and gal *romance* :
She used to come for I to go an' foot it in the dance ;
An' that was werry well jes' then, but when a feller's been
Half o'er the blessed world, yer know, 'ee a'n't no longer
      green !

An' women a'n't ezack loike man, in many ways, yer know,
They keeps the memory of too much as fellers fain lets go ;
They think an' think on what is gone, an' faith, they're slow
      to see
As a boy may 'ave a fancy, an' a man may let it be.

So Cousin Bell was dreadful sore about the trick I played :
She was dreamin' o' them days, ye see, when, as a boy, I
      laid
My head upon her bosom, as she drew me on to do ;
For Cousin Bell was fond on I, an' some years older too.

Ah, an' snakes go crawlin' o'er ye, and spiders big as birds,
An' ants, loike beetles, run in streams—it's far too much
      for words !
An' if ye don't clear out in toime before the winter snows
In werry place ye burnin' were, ye're jes' as loike be froze.

I don't bleeve in Wolseley, wi' his coffee cups an' cans,
An' his Soldier's Pocket-Book an' that on which he boldly
      stan's,

An' tells the British soldier to do his duty clean
On a tea an' coffee ration—oh, he must be jolly green !

I'd loike to see old Wolseley wi his coffee cup and can,
An' nothin' else, a-leadin' up the hills o' Afghanistan ;
I'll swear he'd wish a leetle drop o' summat stronger then,
If he didn' give a glass o' grog to 'earten up his men !

I 'ear as 'ow on Wellin'ton he has bin roight severe
For not pursuin' 'ot'—an' Archie Forbes* made it clear—
But in Cabul, I'm bless'd, *he'd* take a good while to pursue,
An' climbin' at the double on the rocks 'ud turn 'im blue !

He a'n't a' bin among such hills, as far as I do know,
But 'mong the Indians, niggers, an' in Egypt flat and low ;
Well, on them lands the coffee cup and can may make a *do*,
But climbin' at the double on the rocks 'ud turn im blue.

An' what about them boats an' such upon the blessed
         Noile ?—
It fares† to me his ludship found it rayther arduous toil ;
An' didn' care to stay there enny longer than moight be,
Wi' Butlers an' wi' foighten men o' werry hoigh degree !

For one thing I will give him praise—he takes good
         Tommy's part,
In recommendin' on 'im to be precious neat an' smart.
Jes' for to take the ladies' oye, an' 'ave 'is choice an' pick—
It comes by natur'—that do ; so the Gineral spreads it
         thick.

   * Our soldier knows nothing of the refinement of Forbs,
and says distinctly For-bes.
   † Fares—seems, feels.

Yes ; Sir Frederick Roberts led us on—no teapot soldier
     he !—
He knew 'is men, an' made 'em as roight as roight cu'd be;
'Tis true he was ezact an' that, but that a soldier knows
Is the werry ground he can in such his confidence repose !

He's 'is ludship now !—he led us, an' we puts our trust
     in he,
A man among a thousand for 'is pluck an' gallantry ;
An' he never lets 'is men be robbed, as sum ha' been afore,
To profit Jews an' rascals wi' commissions hoigh an' more !

II. TIM JACKSON'S TALE.

(OF PIONEERING LIFE IN AMERICA.)

You guess I've had a cur'ous life, an' roamed i' many lands.
There you are right, I calklate, for 'ere before ye stands
One that has had his brushes with the Indians on the plains,
An' lived for months in swamps that seem'd a-gettin 'tarnal
  rains.

His horses were his only friends among the prairie woods,
Where he wearied for the human voice or even sound of
  floods,
And felt like wishing any change from the ceaseless windy
  swell
That iver rose around and passed, and rose agin and fell.

In wettest Mississippi swamps I've lain for weeks on end,
Far from the reach of letters from a brother or a friend;
And where the crops are wavin' now, I've seen the waters
  shine
For miles and miles on every side in one unendin' line.

And up that very valley when we'd sent the iron horse,
It seemed as if by magic it was drained in proper course;
And what I say for Africa is send a line of rail,
And all along that line will flow a stream that cannot fail—

A stream of civilizin' life that soon brings men and trade,
For the shrill call of the iron horse is sure to be obeyed;
And from remotest ends of earth—as birds for ever go
Where food is full—the folks will come where'er the whistles
    blow.

'Tis wonderful, I guess, and more, to see how round his
    track
There grows the brightest band of white 'longside the line
    of black;
And as the one gets blacker, so the other rises clear,
And spreads till ye have cities—throbbing hearts of hope
    and fear.

That's how we've made Amurrica, away far i' the West;
The States have grown till now, indeed, they're on each
    other prest;
And so 'twill be till every inch of territory's full,
And then poor Europe will, I guess, come here and go to
    school.

I've been awaked at early morn by streams of snakes a-crawl
Across my body on their way to water nigh the fall;
An' there they'd bathe and sport themselves—you'd see the
    water play
In wrigglin' waves about 'em in a sparklin' easy way.

'Twas a trouble, I can tell you, for my dreams got filled of
    such,
And I set my brain a-workin' for to free me from their
    clutch;
And I hit upon the nicest of the tricks I ever tried,
And in one night I nailed them, sir, and made them all go
    wide.

I got me all the hair I could from out my horses' tails,
And gathered more and more until I filled my bags and
        pails;
And then I cut in lengths and ran 'tween strands o' hempen
        rope,
Till all was rough with horses' hairs a-bottom and a-top.

Around my nightly resting-place before I laid me down
I drew this hairy hempen rope, like a wall around a town;
It was the finest fortress, too, against the snakes, you bet;
A smell of that, it was enough—on other paths they set.

The snakes could no more stand it than the cat can mustard
        take;
When they tried to cross, the horses' hair did graze their
        skin and make
Them quickly seek another way; and round they all did go,
A-leavin' me to peace and rest and soundest sleep also.

Cute, wasn't it?—a feller gets right smart when he is thrown
On his resources far away from others, all alone,
With nothing but his horses; and, 'pon my soul, it seems
The very horses get to know their master's thoughts and
        dreams.

There was Abè—so I called him, for our President that died
To give the States a martyr—and he soon became my pride,
An' my safety, too, in danger. He was worthy of his name—
When turned adrift, he'd feed awhile, but back agin he
        came;

Would lay his head beside me till I laid my head on his,
Then, on the slightest stir or sound, I say he'd never miss
To gently move and waken me, and listen—pointing so
With the corner of his one ear, as to say, we'd better go.

An' more'n once 'twas jest in time for me to move away,
For a crowd of 'braves' were on my track jes' at the break
　　　　of day ;
An' when I mounts my Abè, it seemed as if he knew
Exactly how the matter stood, and, like a bird, he flew.

He was worthy of his name, that horse ; I kept him years
　　　　and years,
Till he lost use of his legs and eyes and almost of his ears ;
Then I hires a chap to shoot him, for I couldn't jes' look
　　　　clear,
Or keep the rifle steady on my horse without a peer.

I say as how a man his strength indeed can never know
Till he 'cuts' the town and all the gifts it can on him
　　　　bestow.
He comes to feel his native powers when all alone he goes
Upon the plains and prairies, or the woods around him
　　　　close.

He gets to know time by the sun, and finds his way all thro'
By judging p'ints of compass in the shadows and the dew ;
By smooth sides of the boles of trees, and rosin-weed that
　　　　lays
Its leaves to southward when the sun gives forth its warmest
　　　　rays.

You say it must be cur'ous for to waken in the night
And look upon the silver stars all shinin' on ye bright ?
Yes ; like eyes of mighty giants on ye lookin' kindly down ;
I've often seen 'em, and the twins ezackly like a crown.

The stars are then a comfort, 'tisn them as brings ye fear ;
Ye come to think o' them as friends with gentle eyes and
　　　　clear,

And to know the very worst o' foes are creepin' things and
      frail
Thet bring their slime and venom, too, and allus leave their
      trail.

Down in the Argentine I've roamed through seas of pampas
      grass
When the only thing ye see for miles is the waves that o'er
      it pass ;
And more 'n once I've lost myself, and in despair have found
The track agin by going days all round and round and
      round.

But the wildest of adventures I had down in Mexico,
Where the climate is the very worst that ever I did know.
Ah! 'twas there I met the little gal that took my heart away
All down by Yetchaphetell, where I found myself one day.

She was servin' in a public bar—her father's bar—but there,
'Tis no disgrace in lands like that in work to take a share !
I guess we go for man'ood and woman'ood far more
Than you do in good old England with its peers an' knights
      full store.

She was pretty, slim, her skin as white as pearls in the shell,
Her eyes were black and glancin', her voice was like a bell,
And it set a bell a-ringin' in my heart an' keepin' time
To hers, and so, for once, I let myself go into rhyme.

She showed me many favours, and at last I told my case,
When, to my horror, all the blood deserted her fair face.
She fell back speechless in the chair, and not a word could
      speak,
And I fanned her with my handkerchief and laid kisses on
      her cheek.

She told me thet already she was promised to be wed
To a feller thet had of himself a darn terror made ;
She had listened to his wooing more from fear than any
      love,
An' her father in his fear had come their wooin' to approve.

And as we spoke this feller comes all sudden in the place,
And in the twinklin' of an eye he sees all through the case :
He turns to me and flourishes a bowie-knife in air,
And he cries, ' Clear out, ye blackguard, or the mark of this
      ye'll bear !'

I collared him without a word, and there we went it warm ;
Our bowie-knives played high, and once he cut me in the
      arm ;
The mark of wound you still can see.   My heart was now
      on fire,
And I plunges deep my knife in his, and soon he did expire.

But oh ! the horror of her eyes when at last I caught her
      look
As I rose from off the dead—his blood a-flowin' like a
      brook—
I had to bolt, and ne'er again did little Liza see :
Thet comes o' bein' more expert with knives than one should
      be.

I heard as my poor little gal has ne'er been right again ;—
Gone ravin' o'er that sight she saw, alas ! too clear and
      plain :
The man she loved a murderer of the man as loved her so,
As sich a nature can but love—well, well, 'twas *her* death-
      blow.

I guess thet's how it often goes with fellers jes' like me :
We knock about and get a law unto ourselves, ye see ;
There's good in cities, in so far's ye can't ezackly do
Jes' as you like, and have, perhaps, too many things to rue.

Thet's me : a fellow goin' round incessant seekin' rest—
A clear head an' a heart that burns for ever in his breast ;
And nairy one would fancy now, a-lookin' in my face,
Thet well can smile, I e'er had bin in such a desprit case.

III. CLEAN-SHAVEN.

(A FOX-HUNTING COUNTRY RECTOR'S MUSINGS ON BEING
ORDERED BY HIS BISHOP TO BE CLEAN-SHAVEN.)

WHERE are we now ?   Is't Nineteenth Century's end?
Or go we dreaming back to times of old ?
Here is a missive from our bishop's hand,
Requiring we should tend him cleanly shaved ;
Just think on't ! cleanly shaved, in dapper dress,
White tie, black frock, in formal M.B. cut,
As curates wont to affect in country parts,
To mark them out where naught else would suffice.
Clean-shaven, see you, 'tis as plain as print.
I'm not the man to shave *my* whiskers off
At orders from a fellow chosen so,
Set o'er me by no vote, no word of mine.
And, see you, now my beard is fair and long,
And when I ride to hounds it marks me out
A man of my own type, no more, no less ;
Off-colour I should be without my beard :
The Rector of a Living which I bought ;
Yes, bought, by Jove ! and no man moveth me :
Advowson bought, and, see you, it was cheap,
For the fellow died just in the nick of time,
Though not so old : I got the Living cheap,
And not the *Leaving* dear, as some have done,

Thro' lives prolonged beyond annuitant's mark,
And hope deferred made heavy head, light purse ;
When prize came late and could not be enjoyed.
For mine I did not need for long to wait ;
Here as in other lucky as a Jew.
   ' Clean-shaven,' see you, so the fellow writes,
' Clean-shaven,' bless me, it is come to that :
A set of monkish minkish slaves he'd have,
Pretending to be meek and saintly men.
Why, bless me, look at Jones next parish, see,
A fellow that would sit and booze all day,
His mathematics mazed in whisky fumes,
Till all forgotten his divinity ;
And his divinity is less than mine,
Which, I admit, was never great or free,
With him 'tis lost in mathematics fumed :
Nor difference make on last day of the week ;
His morning service read all husky-voiced,
' The Schriptures movesh us in diversh place,'
That so the *spirit* in his words may tell ;
He read it so 'fore Rural Dean last week,
Like some old Jew just half converted yet,
And strange to all our olden English sounds.
   For what did God upon a man's face set
This ornament, but that it should be worn ?
To mark him out, for manlike though a priest,
To signify his title to the place
That God and Nature gave him. Look you now,
I ride to hounds, 'twas not required of me
To lay my habit down when I went up
For ordination ; nor has it been since,
Nor will be, nor will I shave off my beard.
The fellow fain would utter master be.

No, no; let's go on 'Live and let live' still,
A motto that I favour first and last.
    The patriarchs whose pictures fair we see
Drawn in old books, how reverent of air,
With long beards sweeping freely down their breasts;
And even St. Peter and St. Paul shaved not,
Tho' Paul would fain had all men celibate,
But showed this virile hirsute appendage,
Else all old art doth lie! Jerome himself
Grew splendid beard, and father Cyprian too,
As seen in pictures of the Bolognese.
Look round St. Paul's, and prophets there you see,
And all the apostles carved with ample beards,
And Moses topping all. Why then should we
Seek our examples from a later time,
All weak, and mawkish, and off-colour too:
And follow not the sanctions of the best
Even in the matter of moustache and beard,
But grovel, trying to be monks and friars!
Sad monks and friars, indeed, were some of us;
Or better say, to play them for the nonce.
    And why don't he go barefoot, shave his crown,
Give up his wife and seek the cloister dim,
And there give forth his words? No cloak, nor scrip,
Nor purse! why, where have gone the double fines
We yielded clear for reinstalment claimed
And given? The first for him that died before
He'd filled the seat six moons, and then to this,
That scarce has filled it twenty moons again;
So some will say we were 'clean-shaved' before.
I say reforming should begin at home,
Nor any juggling in this clap-trap way:
We are not saints, not most of us; but vain

And vaunting hypocrites are *some* of us,¹
And in high place we can vaunt the most,   *S*
And all good things of life can still enjoy.
  He sits in's palace, servants at his beck
And call at every hour and minute—see !
And cellars full, wine-stored of choicest brands,
With sunlights at the heart to cheer his days.
The beard is symbol, so the shaving is
A symbol also, not of best but worst ;
And shave I won't, and he may prate till dumb.
  Did Mother Shipton in her prophecies
Not say that when a soldier-bishop came
And walked a monk again, and like a monk
Went bare and bald beneath the eternal sky,
Then England would, indeed, have change on change,
And bad stars rise within her horoscope,
Betokening plague, and fever, pestilence,
Lands wasted of the sun and harvests low,
Men rotting dead on wayside and in waste ?
I'm fain to hold with Mother Shipton there,
And yield not, monkwise—this for country's good ;
Thin end of wedge, and then the evil's done :
Thin end of wedge shall not succeed with me.
  He talks of grace and godly favour too ;
Well, if he wants that why does he go prate
About clean shaving as tho' it lay in that,
The heart and beard I never yet have heard
To rest the one on other.   Luther grew
His beard when that he wisely took to wife,
Why then should I, who am, indeed, no monk
Nor hermit, shave my chin more than my crown ?
Grace, change of heart, I see not lies in that.
No, no ; no razor shall pass o'er my beard,
And his high grace may write until he burst.

*(A few days after, on returning from a meeting at the Rural
Dean's.)*

Clean-shaven ! yes, did e'er you see the like?
The fellows all to barbers' blocks have gone ;
And Jones, e'en Jones, clean-shaven with the rest.
E'en Jones, I say ! Oh, how his hand had shook
When first he laid the razor on his chin,
And how they looked ! a lot of dapper knaves ;
By Jove ! it was a sight to make one weep
To see them look the one on other shaven,
With more than half a smile—a hidden leer—
I really looked a goat among the lambs.
No matter, he will find I'm not the man
To be clean-shaven, lamb-like, monkish-bare.
Even tho' they went on knees to beg me to,
I'd spurn them as the lamb-like knaves they are,
And tell them they are goats tho' void of beard,
And may be I more truly lamb than they,
Albeit beard so long, and red, and full,
For blazon 'gainst them. If I'm coarse by this
That beard be symbol, then I'll e'en be coarse,
And not the smug and shaven hypocrite.

(Later still.)

Reunion ! on my word it seems a farce
To prate of only in our congress hall :
I read of one just lately of our best,
And when the thieves into his cellar broke,
Bore off his finest, so the butler said,
Worth guineas, every bottle, heart of sun.
And all the while do curates starve or no
Down i' the country ? Oh, my God, how fine
A farce it is to see the fellows go

Imping apostles, with their crooks and staves
And fine device heraldic ; mitre too—
The sign of fish-god, Dagon, or maybe
Oannes, just to hint of origin,
Or it may be inheritance of power !
While yet the wretched curates moan and starve !
Phaugh ! and clean-shaved, another fellow holds
The way to make us saints in look, if fact
May not be over-borne.   Reunion still
We need within, first place, and not outside.
When bishops *are* apostles then 'twill be
Millennium clear for one and all of us,
And true Reunion good will come again.

IV. 'ONE O' THE ROIGHT SORT.'

(AN ESSEX BOY'S STORY OF A 'PASSON.')

You say there a'n't no passons now as do their part loike
    men,
A lot o' fellers all for jawr and richual, allus fain
To work the trick all for theirselves, and makes a great
    to-do,
And werry far from sailin' loike a Captain wi' 'is crew.

I'll tell ye o' a chap I knows o' the roight sort for the
    place—
A man as never yet was found a-laggin' i' the race,
When danger was in front, you see, or storms were blowin'
    'ard
Or eppidemics all about, wi' Death writ on the card.

I know he a'n't the man at all to wish hisself in print—
He do his dooty loike a man, and foinds his pleasure in't ;
But that's the werry reason whoy a rhoymin' chap loike me
Should tell the story of his work down yonder by the sea.

Whoy, when the good smack *Alice* she was caught in sudden
    gale,
An' the winds a-blowin' werry wild to shreds had tore her
    sail,

There were some on us were slow to man the loife-boat, for
    we thought,
She ne'er could live in such a sea, no matter 'ow we fought.

Down comes the passon all arrayed in oilskins, lookin'
    grave,
He say, ' My men, we must put out the *Alice* crew to
    save—
We cannot let them perish so within the soight o' land,'
He grasps an oar, and in he jumps, and soon the boat was
    manned.

An' they beat and worked, an' beat and worked, the passon's
    oar went fair—
As sure an' firm as done the oar of any feller there.
An' arter such a foight as made the men breathe 'ard and
    sore,
The *Alice* crew all safe and sound at last was brought to
    shore.

An' when a ship once lay in creek with men all fever
    bound,
An' not a soul to go and say a word of comfort found ;
No sooner do the passon hear of how the poor crew
    fare,
Than he hires a boat, and tells the man to row him quick
    out there.

' Do ye know there's fever on that ship, sir—all the crew are
    down ?'
'Oh yes, I know,' says passon ; 'for I heard on't in the
    town :'

And he goes each day to nurse the men, and spoke the good
      word too,
And say I for one as he's the chap loike Captain to his
      crew.

No sickness, want or death do come to the house of poorest
      man,
No matter if he go to church or bin a careless one ;
The passon's there, and soon he finds good treatment or
      good feed,
Just such as folks in poverty and sickness greatly need.

First time a man was drownded, up in church he puts a
      toile,*
To keep the name aloive, and folks smoiled at it for
      a whoile ;
The werry friends o' drownded man took little notice then,
But allus when such death occurred up went a toile again ;

Till now far round the church, I say, they little tablets
      roise—
A somethin' that recalls so much to mourners' thoughts and
      oyes ;
An' now there's lots o' our folks feel a bit o' church is
      theirs,
An' many go that ne'er before gone there to say their
      prayers.

On All Souls' day there's service, when a lot of folk do go
To church who in the days gone by to move were werry
      slow,
An' allus arter they do say he is a man of men,
An' their children march to church if they do not go there
      again.

      * Tile—an ornamental memorial tablet.

What say ye to *that* passon? a'n't the folks down there in
      luck,
To 'ave a man loike that—a man of downroight faith and
      pluck,
As preaches werry well, but makes his daily practice
      square,
An' wherever ther's distress or that is allus quickly there?

V. ONE OF THE WRONG SORT.

(A WIFE TO HER HUSBAND.)

YES, John, I met him on the street to-day ;
He walked as though he knew next world was made
For him and his—his share assured, complete—
His countenance sharp and clear, and eye so hard ;
Just as I came by Howard's, nigh the church,
He stept across, on seeing me, and made,
To my surprise, up to me ; took my hand
And coldly shook it, as he would excuse
Himself unto himself for such an act ;
And, looking in my face, said, ' Mrs. Rose,
I hope you're well ;' but giving then no pause
For answer, hurried on with these : ' I mourn
For you indeed, within my inmost heart.
You've lost your child ; 'twas hard, 'twas hard for you,
But harder must it be as life goes on ;
For *unbaptized,* no child indeed can be
Accepted of the Saviour—you must hear
For ever rise from depths of hell the cry,
The wail of agony from that poor child
You've doomed to death eternal by neglect
Of Church's service which alone can save ;
Else unregenerate all souls are doomed,

Not even nursling can escape the curse.
I'm sorry for you that must hear the wails
Long as you live within this vale of tears.'
   I stood struck mute: I could do nought but look
Upon his face, clear cut, and on his eye
That seemed to have another eye behind,
That glowed with just a little touch of fire—
It may be of the fire of which he spoke
In tones familiar as he knew it well—
And moisture rose to mine; I could not help—
For strong the image of wee face came back
At words from him.   He saw it, and he said:
'Ah, you may weep, good Mrs. Rose; no soul
Is safe for heaven, save thro' the Church's door,
Her sacraments are all-prevailing there.
Neglect them not next time ; good-day, good-day !'
   I stood a moment where he left me there,
As though a man had stabbed, and I would fall—
A quick rush at the heart, a fluttering pain
Rose upward till my brain seem'd dizzy struck ;
And then, like twig bent back that springs again
Well past its normal, thought came back to me :
'He gathered lambs into His bosom there
In old Judea, though His followers fain
Had scorned them off, and bade the mothers go :
Not so would Jesus ; yes, the babes He *took*
And blessed, and said, My Kingdom is of such,
And never questioned had they formal passed
Thro' all the rule of the Mosaic Law.'
'No, no !' I cried, not such was Jesus' way :
'He *still* may suffer of His followers so
That boldly name themselves elect of His ;
I feel *my* part is in the Master's land,

With child of mine He has in charge for me:
And never priest shall come 'twixt Him and me,
For that I have my dead, a link of grace
Far stronger than their alien sacraments.
I'm rich : and he is poor, despite his scorns,
And claims of right in's service-sacraments ;
He's poor, and hardly yet of Kingdom free,
That Christ declared was made of such as babes.'
And in *this* thought I gained my strength again,
And think of him with pity and with hope,
That some day he may feel he did me wrong,
In lack of human feeling that had wrought
To better issue than his priestly lies.

So be not angry, husband, at his act—
He only showed me where true comfort lies,
When it may be mad sorrow led me wrong—
To thoughts rebellious and to grief too great.

VI. A YORKSHIREMAN IN THE SOUTH.

More easy, lad, ye walk too brisk for me;
Faith, in this part 'tis dry, and I don't drink:
You folk i' South ha' wondrous faculty
For standin' heat, and takin' liquid in:
I niver saw such fellows in my life.
Dry is the land and parched, and yet it grows
Rare corn and wheat, my lad, rare corn and wheat;
But what I like, lad, is to stand a-top
O' Divil's Peak in Darbysheer, you knaw,
Wheer aye some air is stirrin', cool and fresh—
Right cool and fresh in hottest days there be:
The Divil's Peak for me, lad, in the sun
O' summer, when 'tis close and thursty-like,
Or on the moors o' Yorksheer on the rise.
   I niver drink, my lad, I niver drink:
South here, I try to cool me with a hat
I can throw back behind me; and then, see,
My umberella up, lad, then I breathe.
Faith, and they told me waterside was cool,
But there the flies are most uncommon brisk,
And think my bald head was just made for them
And they for it: so now I find a spot
A-top o' railway cutting, where theer stirs

3

A breeze from up the hollow at all hours ;
And theer I sit all snug and cool and nice.
    You want a drink—you have walked well, my lad,
And you may go and get it, while I sit
And see how things are round, lad, things are round.
I like to sit and think while others drink—
I niver spend a pinny in that way,
'The mickle maks the muckle,' so they say
In canny Scotland, and the words suit me—
Though I a Yorksheerman was born and bred ;
Yet there sometimes I've had a treat o' t' drink,
When others paid for 't, lad, when others paid.
    Folks don't respict you, lad, for what you spend
Nor what you give, but just for what ye keep :
You mark it, lad, 'tis what you have and keep
Makes men lift oop their hats, and honour tha ;
You ga and spread it round, and then they think
You are a fool just like unto themselves,
And 'come familiar, sidlin' oop to tha.
No, no, lad, every pinny I can I keep,
And lay them oop, and then i' t' North they say—
'There's Higgie, faith, a warrm man every bit '—
And honour Higgie as both wise and warrm.
    You go and git your drink, and here I'll sit
Even on this binch, lad, and look well around.

    *   *   *   *   *   *

A tidy house it looks and garden trim,
With hollyhocks ranged round in border beds,
An' lookin' at ye as they knaw ye too,
And sunflowers here and there right pert an' gay,
Like likely lass that serves inside, I guess,
To make the fellers joke about and stay.
And lawn in t' middle and the grass well cropped—

And there's the master on t' skittle ground
Preparin' for t' men that coom for t' game;
He is the wise man that mak's skittles pay,
The wise man that; for enny fool can play
And spend his time, his munney, and his strength—
Just to give others power: 'tis t' *power* I'd have,
The power that cooms o' makin' skittles pay;
Aye, that's the little game of life all through!
The lot go play—the one can make it pay;
And he do nowt or little on the job:
Wise men are few; t' fools they go in crowds,
In shoals like fish a-waitin' for the bait.
Here 'tis no cooler; yet see tha how they ga
In tall hats, felts, as thick as sole o' shoe—
All for t' look, or for t' fashion's sake:
And burn theer brains an' niver come to owt:
How could they wi' their brains burned oop to nowt
Wi' sun o' South—that's not the line for me!

   *   *   *   *   *   *

Well, lad, you've got your glass, and now we'll go—
A likely lass that served tha theer inside;
I dinna wonder that tha stayed so lang.
Did ever think, lad, how t' pinnies make
Pounds, and pounds without the little pinnies ne'er
Came into being: the great includes the less:
Lad, pinnies make the pounds tha'lt coom to knaw.
I like to lay them by and soom them oop.
Dang it, the flies are bad as skeetos here:
I would not live in this part for a pound:
I bleeve I'd coom to drink in this part, too.
Joomp ower t' fence fur bit of esh I'll tie
About my yead to keep t' divils off—
They bite down 'ere as if theer drunkards too,

And wouldn't leave a fresh bit o' flesh for owt:
'Tis tender skins, lad, tender skins they find
That yields them sweet, and t' fine blud they knaw:
The coarser folks they niver troubles owt.
　　They're in my room, lad, though I would not say
A word to aunt to vex her kindly sowl,
And oft at night I spend a little time
Before I sleep: with handy pins, ye see,
I settle it may be a dozen or more
And steek them nicely on the wall, and hear
Them buzz and whirl around the fixin' pin
Upon the paper, then I say, 'You're better theer
Than even buzzin, bitin' at my yead.'
We're cautious fellows i' t' North, ye see;
And ne'er let others better us, my lad.
No, nowt so big, nowt little as a fly.
　　You have walked well, my lad, all round wi' me,
And showed me lots, and told me tales enow,
And found my talk and company right good:
If you will lay my maxims in yer yead,
And act upon them, why, lad, you will find
No man e'er gave you better 'largesse' yet:
Good-night and thankee, lad, you've walked right well.

II. ENGLISH RISPETTI.

ENGLISH RISPETTI.

[NOTE.—When I submitted these Rispetti to Mrs. Augusta Webster, asking her consent to my dedicating them to her, as I have done, she wrote to me the following letter, which I print here with her consent, because it has interest and value on the history of English Rispetti:

'I cannot but feel pleasantly flattered that you have dedicated your Rispetti to me. Perhaps I deserve the honour, since I have been the person who "showed the way," as you say, to Rispetti in English, but you are very good to me in your verses bestowing it, and I thank you gladly.

'I made the acquaintance of Rispetti and learned to use the measure by chance while wintering in Florence. I came somewhere, somehow, on the lovely one, "Uccelino che canti per il fresco," learned it by heart, and afterwards tried to translate it line by line, keeping its inversions exactly, which can *almost* be done. Afterwards I got Tommasei's collection, and became familiar with it (I had the pleasure of introducing it to W. B. Scott), but it was only the happening to find my translation of the "Uccelino" in an old portfolio, just when I was stirred up by being in the course of preparing "A Book of Rhyme" for press, that set me off on the delightful task of writing Rispetti myself.

'With this connection of ideas with that Italian bird-rispetto in my mind, it seems to me that your choice of birds as themes for your Rispetti is of quite striking suitability, and yet almost matter of course. To others, to whom bird and rispetto have not the peculiar connection they bear for me, the suitability will hardly be so vividly apparent; but, still, it must be apparent to all. The bright, light creatures, with their wonderful music, seem just made to be sung about in such a way.

'I am sure your Rispetti about them will be liked. And how wonderfully you have observed their different songs. That ought to make them liked as natural history as well as poetry. . . .']

TO MRS. AUGUSTA WEBSTER.

I.

CHIEF of our choir of softer note, yet strong,
  Dramatic-keen, and with the 'lyric cry'
That sweetens, deepens all thy varied song,
  And sense of fate that will not be put by:
Yet joys of love and pathos are with thee
A constant presence, ever radiant, free ;
  To my Rispetti I am fain that thou
  Wouldst give the shelter thou canst well allow.

II.

Thy muse's wing that folds so large a space
  May shadow them, and yield me solace thus
For many blows of fate ; for I can trace
  In thee a spirit kind, magnanimous.
You showed the way : I follow, and am glad ;
And, if I mount no steeps, yet have I had
  A joy in gazing after your ascent,
  And gathering flowerets on the way you went.

SONGS OF THE BIRDS.

I. THE NIGHTINGALE.

SWEET heart of secret minstrelsy—how far
  Thy golden notes, like lightnings in the dark,
Flash full, ebullient, and no rivals mar
  That music flooding all the moonlit park.
Hold, hold, and overpower me not with pain
Of very sweetness ; in thy keen, full strain,
    Notes touch me to the quick—so piercing clear,
    I dream and think a long dead love is here.

II. THE LARK.

Soul of the common field, where grass is green ;
  Melodious voice of morning and of light :
A glory o'er thy path hath ever been,
  With circling radiance in thy upward flight.
Up, up, till lost within the cloudless blue,
While down beneath thy young ones breast the dew.
    Oh, master-singer of our choir ! what glow
    Thou kindlest in the poet's heart below !

III. THE LINNET.

Bird of the moor, where furze and broom rise fair,
   And thistles in their order nod and wave;
Or flax glows whitely to the summer air,
   And where in pools the ousels come to lave:
Sweet singer—soft and low—with fire at heart,
Subdued as tho' by touch of conscious art,
   I love thee well, and in my walks I see—
   Tho' plain—no dearer denizen than thee.

IV. THE WREN.

Like dropping rain upon the parchèd ground,
   Thy song falls sweet on heart and waiting ear;
From tiny throat so full a shower of sound
   Makes marvel in me as I watch and hear:
The jewel of my hedgerow; fain to dart
And brighten all to life; until my heart
   Is grateful that my garden shelter gives
   To sweetest denizen of air that lives.

V. THE BLACKBIRD.

Most mellow flute-notes heard at early morn,
   Before the sun hath risen to flood the ways
With gold; thy matins are with mists upborne:
   First, first of all great nature's hymns of praise.
Oh, minstrel of the morn, like light, thy note
Hath magic as if rolled thro' golden throat.
   More mellow notes no man hath ever heard—
   The soul of poetry in the voice of bird.

VI. THE GOLDCREST.

Thou gracious voice of mid-day, when the heat
   Hath silenced all thy fellowship of song :
Alone thy tiny pulses rise and beat
   The golden air to music all along
In waves of keenest melody intense ;
I muse and doat : a glow within the sense
   Of subtlest joy and pain, like spark that glows
   In fading fire, when wind upon it blows.

VII. THE WHITETHROAT.

Ah, whitethroat ! master of a varied song,
   Chew-rick-a-rew, chew-rick-a-rew, chew-rick,
Repeated all in varied key, till throng
   Thy notes on others : like leaves falling thick
On water softly floating down the stream ;
So softly float thy notes as in a dream
   The current flows, and knows no pause nor rest—
   Such, such the song that stirs thy beauteous breast !

VIII. THE THRUSH.

Bird of the liquid note that grows and swells,
   Repeated till the rapture rises clear,
And all around is thrilled, as tho' there dwells
   A melody within the atmosphere :
How oft when sunset glorious dies away
I've heard thee sing the requiem of day ;
   And twilight gathered round thee gray and pale,
   And thou sang'st on as tho' thou *wouldst* prevail.

IX. THE GARDEN WARBLER.

Sweet, sweet in bosom of the wood to hear
    In drowsy afternoon the warbler's lay;
Soft rise the mellow notes, then piercing clear—
    It adds a grace to summer's loveliest day.
My warbler of all warblers first and best—
My garden warbler near his low-set nest,
    Discoursing music to his mate and me
    As lone I sit at root of alder tree.

X. THE BLACKCAP.

Right o'er and o'er again he tells his tale
    With fiery fervour to the trees and streams :
A full keen pipe that never yet did fail
    Of something to recall long-vanished dreams.
He speaks to youthful days when first was heard
His deep wild note, yet sweet, and of the bird
    A very part, his song is one with him :
    You see him black-capped in the shadow dim.

XI. THE SWALLOW.

How sweet to me when round the cottage eaves
    Are heard thy twitterings in the mornings clear,
When all around are stirrings in the leaves
    And distant notes of many birds I hear.
But thou art nearest, and thy song is sweet :
Image of faith and constancy complete :
    Thou, with thy mate, returnest year by year,
    With grateful message both to see and hear.

XII. THE ROBIN.

Bird of the youthful fancy and of love,
    Because ye did the leaves on dead babes strew,
When all was real and nothing could us move
    Far from the lights of olden tales we knew ;
Ah ! and thy song is of the young world still—
All childlike pathos in thy notes does thrill—
    Sweet mendicant, that haunts my kindly door,
    And pays with music for thy little store.

XIII. THE CUCKOO.

Voice of the spring, repeated o'er and o'er ;
    I lie and listen pleased to that one word,—
Cuckoo ! Cuckoo ! that rises more and more,
    Till all my pulses once again are stirred.
For in the days gone by oft did I stray
With one no more, and listen to thy lay.
    And now I walk alone ; and as I hear
    Thy note, unbidden comes once more the tear.

XIV. THE CHAFFINCH.

A spirit haunts my garden, morn and eve,
    And sweetly shakes his song from yonder tree ;
I see him oft, for seldom does he leave
    The little corner where his loved ones be.
See, there he flies, and settles on that spray,
Pours out his sweet but sudden closing lay.
    He is not strange, nor would a stranger be ;
    I joy to have him of my garden free !

XV. THE BLUE TIT.

He passes me like bit of wingèd sky—
 A bird of wondrous beauty, heart of hope ;
And drops his little notes so fair, that I
 Would fain he'd take himself a larger scope :
Sweet bird, I sit and patient watch and hear
Thy converse with thy mate in accents clear :
 A joyous radiance to thy wings belong,
 If thou art not the master-chief of song.

XVI. SPARROWS.

Brave birds, and busy in my limes and round
 My outhouse eaves all seasons of the year ;
How oft at sunrise have I heard the sound
 Of your keen voices, penetrating clear :
Clear, steely, full of joy, and with the sense
Of some profound and cheerful innocence ;
 Brave birds, from you I fain would learn the way
 To make the most of chances every day.

XVII. THE WATER OUSEL.

Oft have I seen him, like a flash of light,
 Go past me as I lingered on the edge
Of brooklet, where the water soft and bright
 Flowed over stones and murmured in the sedge.
On stone he'd sit, then dive, return again,
And pipe so fair I could not but remain,
 And listen to his song, so passing sweet,
 And wish and wish he would that tale repeat.

XVIII. THE STARLINGS.

High overhead they fly in autumn eve
   In band compact, and, as they onward go,
Drop notes and cries so strange, you would believe
   They had some tale to tell you fain would know.
' Philosophers among the birds,' are they;
And if less sweet than others in their lay,
   They seem to know so much and keep it still—
   Birds of rare prudence and fine force of will.

XIX. THE STARLING'S SONG.

' Less sweet than others !' did you never hear
   His notes rise fair from wall or olden tree,
When that his mate breasts pale-blue eggs so clear,
   And other's notes enrich his melody ?
You could believe he sang 'twixt laugh and sigh ;
His joy is such he cannot all pass by
   The fun he finds in nature and in life—
   The sage of birds, he jests amid the strife.

XX. THE BULLFINCH.

How oft I've mourned men's hands against thee bent—
   Sweet visitor, and welcome to my store ;
What matters if thou art on buds intent,
   Thou richly pay'st me for them o'er and o'er ;
For sometimes lowly piping in my trees
Thy notes drop gently ; surely hard to please
   Were he that did not feel his heart uplift,
   When thou hast sung thy song—a precious gift.

XXI. THE GOLDFINCH.

My favourite of finches, bird so rare !
    I love to see thee seek my corner wild
Where thistles grow, and weeds that still are fair
    Though some would hold my garden all defiled.
Soft are thy notes when in the sunlight clear
They rise, and softly fall upon my ear
    All unexpected—sweet, yet full of fire.
    O bird, of that song I would never tire !

III. NARRATIVE AND LYRICAL.

I. THE GREAT KHALIF'S CONFESSION.

[Abd-er-Rahman III. ascended the throne of the Moorish empire in Spain when a mere youth of twenty. He at once set himself to repair the confusion into which the kingdom had fallen in the hands of weak predecessors. He subdued the recalcitrant Arab usurpers who had fastened on parts of the empire; he made the rebellious Christians submit; fortress after fortress fell; and in the midst of success he never abused his power. Mr. Stanley Lane-Poole, in his 'Moors in Spain,' thus writes of him:

'The Moorish historians describe this resolute man in colours that seem hardly consistent with his strong, imperious policy: nevertheless, they describe him faithfully as the mildest and most enlightened sovereign that ever ruled a country. His meekness, his generosity, and his love of justice became proverbial. None of his ancestors ever surpassed him in courage in the field and zeal for religion. He was fond of science, and the patron of the learned, with whom he loved to converse. Many anecdotes are told of his strict justice and impartiality.'

He made Cordova, after Byzantium, the most beautiful of cities then existing. The great work of his later years (outside the toils of government, which he never in any sense deputed to others) was the building of the great palace of Ez-Zahará (The Fairest) in honour of the best loved of his wives, and named after her. He was devotedly attached to her, and she once begged him to build her a city, which should be called after her name, which he did; having all his life had great delight in building.

After his death a paper was found in the Khalif's own hand-
writing, in which he had carefully noted those days in his long
reign in which he had been free from all sorrow: they numbered
only fourteen. 'O man of understanding,' he added, 'wonder
and observe how small a portion of unclouded happiness the
world can give even to the most fortunate.']

ABD-ER-RAHMAN sat in his ivory chair
Thinking of palaces, stately and fair,
From which he might gather a hint of grace,
To aid him some worthier line to trace
In the palace he now was fain to design
To honour Ez-Zaharā of grace divine—
The first of his wives for beauty, and more—
For sweetness and truth, and the love she bore.
And there rose in fancy the images fair
Of towers and domes in the clear blue air,
With their crests whereon the crescent would gleam,
Reflecting the sunlight like faëry dream.
His mind as he sat, by the strangest law,
Went travelling back with a sense of awe,
O'er the years that had passed since, young and bold,
He mounted the throne of the Emirs old:
When he grasped the reins of a falling state,
And proved restoration was not too late,
That the sceptre which weakling hands had swayed,
All unworthy those who the kingdom made,
With the sense that the Prophet, sent of God,
Was with them to lighten their heavy load,
In the hands of a man of might and will
Might blossom and flower, as aforetime, still.
   He thought of his labours by sword and pen,
Of the wars well waged with rebellious men:
Of battles and sieges, and sudden surprise,

When the waves of revolt, like seas, did rise:
Of the hours of thought, the sagacious plan,
The perilous charges, himself in the van,
By the which he secured the kingdom's peace,
And had fixed the laws that gave rich increase—
Till the Moorish power had risen again,
And for tears given smiles unto sunlit Spain,
And wealth that was better than warlike spoil—
Content and abundance of wine and oil:
Till the downtrode Spaniards once more were free
From the lash of the Arab nobility;
And robber and brigand no more could rove,
And ravish the fruits of the field and grove:
Till even the Christians confest it good
To honour a king that no foe withstood;
Who had equal justice for sovereign goal,
And built up the fragments to one grand whole.
And the cares of empire so sore had weighed,
He felt for success in his soul he paid.
His joy he had yielded that Spain might smile,
And its valleys be rich in wine and oil;
Where the mosque and temple not far apart
Heard the prayer in each from the fervent heart,
And the 'Allah, mashallah,' rising clear,
In the Christian wakened no sense of fear.
　　He knelt as the Azan rang overhead;
When again he arose, he mused and said:
'The king, be he chosen or born as heir
To the throne, must the people's burden bear:
His life he must give for the good of all,
If he strive to follow the nobler call:
No rest can remain for the head that guides,
Nor the heart with room for a world besides

The personal need, and is fain to rise
To the law eternal that guides the wise.
How few of the days of my changeful life
Have been free from care and unvexed of strife !
From the one care forth still another sprang,
·And the same sad tune under all there rang
In my ears : Nothing holds : all yields to change,
Whether still we stand, or more boldly range :
I have ceaseless laboured and sought the good
Of the vagrant and self-willed multitude,
Who believe that I, in this chair of state,
With the bowing crowds that upon me wait,
Must indeed be happy and free from care,
And enjoy old age, with the amplest share
Of friendship and honour and cheerful rest,
With no cloud of trouble to dull the breast.
Alas, and alas ! they but judge by shows.
If I count my gains to the latest close,
My joys I scarcely can reckon so high
That I need much to boast of my destiny :
Of the changeful days of my busy life,
I find but a few are unmarred of strife ;
Or changes or death, or the sense of loss,
Or the darkening shadow of some cross.
    ' But the palace shall all the fairer be,
For love finds its joy in extremity.
In dangers it knows, and the risks it runs,
And labours that grow with the lessening suns,
Ez-Zahará shall shine on high, and tell
To all future time that I loved as well
As planned, thought and conquered, and ruled, and gave
Laws that were fruitful to yield and save.
And perchance in the years when Spain hath ceased

To share in the joys of the well-spread feast
Of a faithful rule, and is forced to bow
To a weaker sceptre than rules it now,
Ez-Zaharā will still remain to tell
Abd-er-Rahman's wish was to rule it well ;
And when, with wonder, the travellers gaze
On the golden domes, and the winding ways,
On the pillared courts, and the fountains fair,
And the rich mosaics of colours rare :
On the spires that shine, and the crests that glow,
And the gates with their richly-carven show,
They will say Abd-er-Rahman of lion heart
Found gain in the beauty of love's own art ;
And he spread over Spain his tokens true
Of a love that with time ever waxed and grew :
And softened his rule and so made it great ;
For love is the power that upholds a state,
As it holds the heart of a man and makes
Even weak souls stronger for others' sakes '

Oriental Record.

II. 'DETTIN' A BID BOY NOW.'

Two little fellows, with their noses pressed
Against the pane, not more than four years old;
Arms round each other's necks, and poorly clad,
Dirty in hands and face, and down at heel,
Their little legs exposed, but smiling sweet,
Stood, watching birds within birdseller's shop
In dingy London street, as I passed by.
A something in their air caught, made me pause
Beside; and, listening, kindest words I heard
Addressed to little birds that could not hear.
'Ah, pretty! what's de time? tweet-tweet,' and then
'Would like tum sugar, oh now, wouldn't oo?'
'Dettin' a bid boy now, just ain't oo, though.'
And on through round of quaint remarks like these,
That erst their elders had addressed to them,
Repeated oft, with many a change, and 'tweet'
Varied through quite an unexpected range;
'Dettin' a bid boy now, just ain't oo, now?'
And 'Would oo like tum sugar or a trumb
O' mudder's bread: we wish we 'ad it 'ere,
Dear 'ittle birdies, oo so pretty—tweet,
An' can't det out, dear 'ittle birdies—tweet!'
   And there they stood, and chattered to the birds,
That leaped and looked right curiously at them,

Though not a sound could any birdie hear ;
Yet was it sweet to see the children seek
To cheer the birdies in their childish way ;
And in their wish to cheer the birdies there,
Unknowing, also cheered me as I stood
And listened, while the roar went ever on—
The misty roar of London's crowded streets.
  Who would not wish such kindly sense maintained
To brighten life, and draw the childish heart
Up into manhood, with its fair sweet light,
To make the man true man in gentle art,
To comfort even the little birdies there
With words of all goodwill and graciousness ?

III. FOR THE PRINCESS MAY.

(*May* 19, 1893.)

As sometimes misty clouds that, rolling dun,
Have darkened earth, but, passing near the sun,
Caught glory of the ray, and shown a splendour
That to the watching eye was welcome, tender:
So now the cloud, transformed to radiance, turns
Its side to us that with the sunshine burns;
The joy of marriage-bells in prospect stirred,
Above the noise of every day is heard.

O Princess, may thy fate be always such;
The cloud transformed by ever-mellowing touch
Of blissful Time, and from the mists arise
A new and radiant glory of the skies,
To make to glow the former weeping eyes.

Happy be thou as bride and wife, serene:
Stillness of joy as e'er on earth hath been—
A patient spirit ever-seeking new
The works of gracious bounty to pursue:
A kindly purpose that can ever find
Solace in helpfulness to human kind.

Be happy in thy love, and find but more
Of vantage in the good that cheered before,
Till all can see the queenly spirit rise
To all the blissful human ministries :
As bride and wife may peace and gladness crown
The broadening life that all the world shall own.

Atalanta.

IV. IN CROCKLEFORD WOOD IN AUTUMN.

LET critics taunt me as they may,
　　Dear Crockleford, I yet have you :
My mistress sweet, and smiling gay,
　　All radiant with the morning dew.

Lone in the heart of wood I lie
　　And listen to a murmurous sound :
Surely some living breath passed by,
　　And stirred the leaves and kissed the ground.

I feel it not upon my brow,
　　Or hand when I uplift it—so ;
But, see, the ferns are stirring now
　　From golden frond to root below.

A mighty hand has toucht them there,
　　A hand that warms their inmost core ;
And so they beat with pulsings fair
　　In circling movements more and more.*

For every bud and leaf has played
　　Its part to perfect all the rest ;
And none for self alone has laid
　　Its treasure up within the breast.

　* In reference to Darwin's discovery that every part of every
leaf is making ceaseless circling movements in the air.

Oh, sweetest bond in nature's life—
   The perfect law of 'give and take,'
The law that still subdues all strife
   To one accord, without a break.

And there beside me rises fair
   The primrose of the autumn time:
Oh, sacred is its beauty rare,
   Beyond the beauty of the prime.

And later violet, soft and shy,
   Looks out as if with wonder too:
All childhood in its little eye,
   All heaven within its tender blue.

How sweet to rest and muse and dream,
   And wonder if that sound and swell
Are half in fact and half but seem,
   And never will their secret tell.

Let critics taunt me as they may,
   Dear Crockleford, I yet have you:
My mistress sweet, and smiling gay,
   All radiant with the morning dew.

October 13, 1893.

V. A DIRGE

FOR THE BRAVE WHO WENT DOWN IN THE 'VICTORIA.'

I.

WEEP for the fallen brave
That sleep beneath the wave,
In a vast unmeasured grave,
    Far within the Syrian Sea ;
Whose funeral knell is rung,
And their last sad requiem sung
    By ocean-winds that wander free.

II.

No mourners there may stand,
And clasp each other's hand,
As they think of that brave band
    Who lie at rest below ;
No tear of grief may fall
On their ever-shifting pall
    Of mighty ocean-waters as they flow.

III.

Nor wife, nor lover, friend,
O'er their last sad bier can bend
With sweet soothing, as they lend

Their loving look and touch to the dead :
No satisfying farewells,
Nor the sigh nor kiss that tells
    The stricken hearts are comforted.

IV.

Yet they sleep secure of fame ;
They have won an honoured name,
And their memory shall claim
    Tender thoughts and many a tear :
With the true heroic heart
They stood to do their part,
    And met their fate without a fear.

V.

With brave Kempenfeldt and those
Who with him went to repose :
With the men whose ranks did close
    As the *Birkenhead* went down :
Our brave brothers shall be named,
They shall never be defamed,
    They have won a high and beautiful renown.

VI.

To be enshrined a part
Of a mighty nation's heart,
With the tenderness of art,
    Is their high and glorious meed ;
To be forgotten never
As the nation grows forever,
    And to aid it evermore in its need.

Scotsman.

VI. A DREAM.

(AFTER READING THE NEW AND REVISED EDITION OF PROFESSOR J. VEITCH'S 'HISTORY AND POETRY OF THE SCOTTISH BORDER.')

OH, sweet the morning air,
As I lightsomely did fare
To the faëry land of Ercildoune where the Rhymer Thomas
    lay;
And all the trees in trance
Seemed to waver and to dance,
As clear before me came in view the green and winding way.

And a bower before me rose
Set sweet in green repose,
And within it sat the wizard with a gentle look and gay:
His face was soft and mild:
He had eyes like to a child,
Although his brow was wrinkled, and his hair was waving gray.

'Ye are come with me, to see
The things that yet may be.'
And he held before my wond'ring eyes, while he most
    sweetly smiled,
A little glassy sphere,
And within it did appear
The vision of a country that was neither soft nor wild.

But a blending of the two :
And a stream went wandering thro',
With the sweetest music ever yet that rose to human ear ;
And I said, 'What stream is this,
That sings like soul in bliss?'
And he said, 'The stream is Yarrow, that to history shall
be dear.

'There the dreams of men shall meet
With a longing soft and sweet,
And pilgrims from afar shall come to hear its music low,
And poets oft shall sing
Of the loves that round it cling ;
For the passion and the pathos of the past shall crown it so.

'The mystery and the dream
Of the poet still shall seem
To hang o'er all its borders, in the shadows soft and low,
In the springtime of the year,
In the lights of summer clear,
And over all shall ever shine the great Magician's glow.

'The flowers of Yarrow bloom
For ever, and the tomb
Can never kill their memory, nor rob them of their youth ;
Oh, the life we live is dream—
Things are not as they seem ;
For 'tis love, and song, and phantasy that clothe the world
with Truth.'

'What is that lofty tower
With bastions that lower
O'er the steep that seems to darken beneath the shadows
    gray?'
    'Oh, that is Newark proud
    Where the tide of war has bowed
And risen, and swept in circles round in red and lurid play.'

    'And what is this I see?'
    As he turned the sphere to me,
'Oh, what is this so lovely as it rises on the height,
    Like enchanted castle fair,
    Or a battlement in air?'
'Oh, that is Neidpath where the maid did die in love's
    despite.'

    'And what is this?' I cried,
    'Comes from the other side?'
'Oh, that is Ashiestiel,' he said, 'where a wizard true shall
    dwell;
    He yet shall full restore
    All the Border love and lore,
And for the future from the past shall bring the master spell.'

    'And what is this I see—
    In the midst a green birk-tree?'
'The Bush aboon Traquair,' he said, 'where lovers did con-
    vene;
    And bards in many a strain
    Will tell the tale again
Of the sweet, sweet love that pledged its vows beside the
    birk sae green.

'And in songs their love shall live
Thro' the ages, and shall give
A charm and wonder to the scene to make the bosom thrill,
And Shairp repeat the tale,
In words that will not fail,
Of the bush that grew where lovers ance their cup o' love
did fill.'

'And what hill do I see
That looks like one yet three?'
'Oh, that is Eildon's triple height with lights that glow and
dance;
A wondrous hill to rise
Triple-pointed to the skies,
And hoary with its legends, its glamour, and romance.

'There King Arthur dreaming lies;
And his knights, with wondering eyes,
Are waiting for the fuller time when back they come again,
To fight the greater fight,
And once more to spread the light
Of chivalry; and Merlin raise a yet more kindling strain.

'Yes, they wait and, longing, dream
Of the magic and the gleam
That Merlin ever saw before but dimly shaped and fair;
Oh, they wait, and long, and see
Many things that yet shall be,
And I with them shall counsel take, when I am wafted there.

'For within the Eildon Hill,
    Far removed from storm and ill,
There they rest, and, wondering, wait for the greater time
    to be,
        And all who journey there,
        Look on their peaceful air,
And know that they will waken to make our world more free.'

'And, oh, what wondrous scene
    As on earth hath never been,
With a light that wavers o'er it that nor moon nor sun can
    know;
        Where a stream of living light,
        Like a water flows in sight,
And from it rise for ever faëry forms that come and go?'

'Oh, that's the fair life-tide,
    Flowing ever soft and wide,
In the which the sweet Kilmeny for fuller life did lie:
        This is the faëry land
        On the bounds of which I stand:
Oh, hark the call! it comes for me: I would not put it by.

'Oh, hark, how soft and clear—
    See, the hart and hind appear!
They follow each the other close as signal I must go;
        See the elfin folk that wait
        To bear me off in state
To their native land of wonder far beyond all men can know.

' Beneath the Eildon Hill
With its triple peaks so still,
Lies the door into the elfin land where now I follow fain ;
And when I come once more
Back to earth, for ever sore
My heart will long for elfinland and hear its magic strain.'

*   *   *   *   *

Then the Rhymer's eye grew dim—
Deep sleep did fall on him :
For the Queen of Elfinland to her had called him far away—
To her land of wondrous light
Nor of moon nor sun so bright :
And I awoke and found that I in bed in London lay.

VII. MEMORIES.

I.

My love he went to Burdon Fair,
And of all the gifts that he saw there,
Was none could his great love declare ;
So he brought me marjoram smelling rare—
Its sweetness fillèd all the air.
    Oh, the days I dote on yet,
    Marjoram, pansies, mignonette !

II.

My love he sailed across the sea,
And all to make a home for me.
Oh, sweet his last kiss on the lea,
The pansies pluck'd beneath the tree,
When he said, ' My love, I'll send for thee !'
    Oh, the days I dote on yet,
    Marjoram, pansies, mignonette !

III.

His mother sought for me anon ;
So long my name she would not own.
Ah, gladly would she now atone,
For we together make our moan !
She brought the mignonette I've sown.
    Oh, the days I dote on yet,
    Marjoram, pansies, mignonette !*

Good Words.

    * This piece has twice been set to music.

VIII. LOOKING BACK.

IT's oh for the sunny stream
  That leaps by the daisied lea !
And it's oh for the cot by the wood
  Where my good man first brought me !

I walk up and down among silk,
  And servants come at my call,
And my hands are whiter than milk ;
  But I mourn in midst of it all.

It's oh for the cot by the wood,
  The smoke curling up to the west,
The working and waiting and looking forth
  For a face to bring me rest !

Tender looks it has for me still—
  It is gentle and true as of old ;
But 'tis hard to have no skill,
  And a brain that won't take hold !

I try and strive till I faint,
  And wish I could only lie
Always asleep, and dream that I live
  In the happy days gone by.

It's oh for the sunny stream
  That leaps by the daisied lea !
And it's oh for the cot by the wood
  Where my good man first brought me !

Good Words.

IX. LIGHT AND SHADOW.

*' Unto you that fear my name shall the Sun of Righteousness
arise with healing in His wings.'—Mal. iv. 2.*

THE old cathedral rises hoar,
    And lifts its lofty towers
Above the ceaseless whirl and roar
    That fill the market hours;
When from the wealthy country round
    The crowds come trooping in
To buy and sell and make exchange,
    And golden wealth to win.

And till the sun stoops to the west,
    Apace the current flows—
A scene of bustle and unrest,
    From opening to the close;
And when the stir subsides again,
    The shadows deepen down,
And fall on eave and niche and wall,
    And hide the gurgoyle's frown.

But upward creeps the sunlight,
    To rest on tower and spire,
Their gilded summits twinkling bright,
    As if alive with fire.

And so above our daily life,
    When vexed with little cares,
Our souls may raise themselves on high,
    Amid those heavenly airs

That blow about our common life,
    To keep it pure and strong,
And catch the light of that blest Sun
    To whom life doth belong,
And hold it forth a witness clear
    To those in sin that lie,
That over all the changes here
    We see a Light on high.

Sunday Magazine.

X. FLOWERS AND HYMNS.

[On hearing some children on a Sunday afternoon playing on the piano and singing snatches of hymns, unconscious of being heard, which led a friend, as he pointed to the primroses and violets that adorned the table in the room where we sat, to say: ' Flowers are the hymns of nature, and hymns are the flowers of the religious life.']

FLOWERS, in truth, are hymns of nature :
　　From the common earth they rise ;
Rich of fragrance, fair of feature,
　　Drinking dews of heavenly skies.

All of sweet they bring or brighten—
　　Joy to youth and hope to age ;
Heavy hearts they oft may lighten
　　Tender memories to engage.

Days of childhood, wandering graces
　　Of the world when all was young
The earth still full of angel faces,
　　Known and loved, though yet unsung.

Hymns are truest flowers of fragrance,
　　From fair souls that softly rise
Above the common soil with radiance,
　　Holding converse with the skies ;

Drinking dew of soft communings,
   Mystic, pure, and shedding bliss,
With the glow of high attunings
   To a nobler life than this.

So, children, play, oh, still play on,
   Though with a faltering note, and sing :
Like random winds on air-harps blown
   Our hearts are moved, and tribute bring.

XI. JUNE.

OH, the balmy woodland
   In the month of June !
Never did the birds sing
   Sweetlier in tune !
Rich the roving blossoms
   Hang from branch and spray ;
'Tis an ever-new delight
   The live-long day.

Sweet surprises meet us
   Everywhere we turn ;
Blue-bells like bonnie eyes
   Peeping thro' the fern.
Half we grudge to gather
   Beauties that we prize,
But we seek for offerings
   To gladden weary eyes.

Good Words.

XII. DECEMBER.

WHITE are the fields, white-robed are the firs,
Deep is the quiet; not a breath of wind stirs.
The world seems, by magic, all muffled and still,
As if frozen to picture, both lowland and hill.
The moon casts a mellowy light over all,
And afar, like a whisper, the sound of the fall
Is caught by the ear that, listening intent,
Might think it the voice of one, toiling and spent,
And calling for aid, as the owl's lonely cry
Makes start the belated poor man passing by,
With his bundle of faggots, to keep the keen cold
From invading the tenderer lambs of his fold;
And the sportsman, returning with dog at his heel,
Begins—even he—the sharp frost-breath to feel,
And, beating his hand upon his cold breast,
Surprises the birds half asleep in their nest.
Our God He is scattering His morsels so fine
That the earth may be clothed with a raiment divine,
To guard it, and make it yield harvests again
When past are the seasons of snow-drift and rain.

Sunday Magazine.

XIII. SERENADE.

I.

Away the black night flies
   Before the shafts of day ;
Faintly the firstling beams arise
   And shimmer on meadows gay.
   What dream'st thou, maiden, say,
At the window all alone ?
     Is it in the night
     Thy heart is light ?
Ah, would it were mine own !

II.

Oh, richly the roses twine
   Around thy trellised walls !
Thou seest them quiver and shine
   When the faint beam on them falls :
   So my love-thought never palls
As it goes to you from me :
     A roselet fair
     With dew-tears rare.
Oh, dare I bring it thee ?

III.

The soft south wind upsprings
  To embrace the earth as it wakes ;
Like sound from a dove's soft wings
  Are the gentle sighs it makes.
So, maiden, my thought close clings
  To thy image fair as a dream :
    Is it in the night
    Thy heart is light,
When things are not as they seem ?

IV.

For the morning, south wind, rose,
  Are emblems alike of thee,
And within my heart there glows
  The thought of thy fancies free,
And of all the pure heart knows
  Of Love's great mystery :
    A roselet fair
    With dew-tears rare.
Oh, dare I bring it thee ?

XIV. THE SPARROWS' WINTERING.

When the oaks are bare and leafless,
   And the autumn shows are past ;
When the hips and haws and ivy
   And the hollies radiance cast ;
When across the fields and meadows
   Blows the cold November blast ;

When at night the mists do gather
   On the hedges in the lane ;
And at morn, when twilight glimmers,
   Trees are traced upon the pane,
And the lads go forth to look
   For ice to slide on once again ;

When the hoar-frost lies like silver
   On the grass, a lacework fine,
Making all the twigs and branches
   Rich in chaste and fair design,
And the black and wasted tree-stumps
   Show a soft aerial line ;

When the robin, crimson-breasted,
  Comes once more to door and sill,
Trustful, looking for the morsels
  Ever given with right goodwill;
And the blackbird, bolder grown,
  Comes close and shows his golden bill :

Then the sparrows that had chattered
  Thro' the brighter summer days
Round about the homestead freely,
  Twittering their cheerful lays,
Gather in their crowds for winter
  In their own appointed ways.

See, they come in varied flocks
  To swell the pretty feathered throng ;
Come from east and west to shelter
  In the winter drear and long,
And in little breaks of sunlight
  Lighten winter with a song.

Thus the little sparrows bring
  A lesson for the darkened days :
To draw together close and warm,
  To seek our cheer in social ways,
To aid and shelter each the other,
  And in love find all our praise.

IV. SONNETS.

I. WHY NO LOVE-SONGS?

(TO A FRIEND WHO EXPRESSED SURPRISE THAT MY
VOLUME CONTAINED NO LOVE-SONGS.)

I.

My friend, let others sing of love
   Who lightly move through measures gay :
   I am not fain to turn that way,
And know I could not all improve

The *sweet, sweet* lays of those that move
   In circles as the Cupids play,
   And in delightful gardens stray,
' Long drinks ' to drain—all sweets above.

Had I e'er known such bosom throes,
   Such yearnings of a fervid youth,
To such a height I might have rose ;
   That cup is emptied now, in truth.
      What good to stir exhausted fires—
      Say ashes burn when flame expires ?

II.

Of love they only ought to sing
　Who still enjoy and flutter gay
　In sunlight fair upon the way;
Their life a still unclouded spring!

For me no more, I mount on wing
　Of passion; and no more can say,
　If kiss be sweet, embrace be gay,
Or well 'long drinks' to drain, and sing.

Like bird with wing all clipped and bare
　I lie and look, but cannot rise;
　Or 'mid the dust I drudge with cries
　All vain, though still in maiden's eyes
I read the secret hidden rare
That tells me love may yet be fair.

III.

But which the love that should be sung?
   The love that is but hot unrest—
   That drains 'long drinks' from beauty's breast,
And only knows the changes rung

On such delights, and oft hath flung
   Defiance at hard fate and more?
   Or is't the love that oft hath bore
Neglect or scorn and curbs the tongue,

And purifies itself, and grows
To greater as new life it knows,
   Enlarging still the self-control :
Gains sense of fuller will : repose :
And never knows an earthly close,
   Yet reaches life serene and whole?

IV.

Ah, love may grow by cravings sweet !
   For love denied and ne'er confest,
   Made purer thro' the hopeless quest ;
Which fair success might all defeat.

The paradox of life we meet
   Just here ; love lives without return,
   And may more clearly, purely burn
Veiled, as in lamps sepulchral, sweet.

And blame me not, I pray you, here
   If I no love-song bring you now ;
For these, with what they have of cheer,
   Are all too well supplied, I vow :
      I would not ape them if I could ;
      I could not ape them if I would.

II. READING MY POEM-BOOK.

I.

SOMETIMES I read my book, and feel a glow
   As if a light struck clear across the page
   That would my heart and fancy full engage ;
And then again the light dies down, and low

A shadow creeps as on a dial, slow,
   And darkens every line ; and then I wage
   A war against myself until the page
Is like a face that, mocking, scorns, and so

I close it in despair, and turn away
   To seek some comfort in another's mind,
And wonder if *there* is indeed the play
   Of my own fancy, or, if only blind,
I was indeed a feeble castaway—
   The voice of something alien and unkind.

II.

Ah me ! and is it that a man is slave
  Of some familiar spirit that doth lead
  Him on and on in straitened ways decreed,
When that he deems he need not freedom crave ?

Oh, folly of fond hope that will not save
  A shade of comfort for my mournful need,
  And then, behind the page, gives me to read
Lines as on death's-heads carved to make me rave !

Did I not think in singing I had found
  Some faint relief from all the world of care ?
  Alas ! and now I blindly forward fare
With more of conscious burden on my round ;
  For to the heavy burden that I bear
  Is added grief that I have shown my wound.

III.

Oh, mocking forms that sometimes to me brought
   The show of comfort when my heart was fain
   To find some cheer if others read my strain,
And felt with me and shared my plaintive thought.

Delusions all ! what matters that I wrought
   To verse the echo of my utter pain ?
   It now but mocks me as with one refrain :
' Fool, fool ! from others *thus* help to have sought !'

What then, if many unto whom I sent
   My book, despise it, or decline to read,
   They render unto me the self-same meed
I render to myself, and this way spent,
   I hate myself and blame them not at all,
   And wish I could my every gift recall.

IV.

That they of me might know nought nor recall
    That which I once deemed fair confession true ;
    That I might die from them and never rue
My friendly gifts so free to one and all.

I am not worthy praise to me should fall :
    I seek it not, and thank them they despise
    The token I had held before their eyes
With no desire that I should them enthrall :

But only show I laid some store on this—
    That I had been with Pain upon his peak,
And with great Death exchanged one solemn kiss
In token that with him lay all my bliss :
    I would not any more from others seek
    Such aids as show them strong and I all weak.

V. FAMILIAR OF GREAT DEATH.

For now I *am* familiar of great Death :
  With him I pace the ever-narrowing ways
  Where, in the shadow, Hope's fair finger lays
A light, and Love gives quickness to the breath.

And ever as we go, Imagination saith :
  ' How were it if, with Death, all Love could die ?'
  Nay, Love that was, still lives, I make reply :
What hath been is, and ' Love fulfilled of Faith.'

We cannot walk by sight : Love seeks its own,
And finds, even tho' our world be overthrown :
We seek the light that erst before us lay,
  And find but shadow and our hearts are sore ;
  For that we find not as we found before ;
And, lo ! are drawn to life the backward way.

III. SEVEN SONNETS TO MY FRIENDS:

RECIPIENTS OF 'THE CIRCLE OF THE YEAR.'

I.

To *some* of my 'friends,' who failed to acknowledge the free
New Year's gift of my volume, or did so in merely perfunctory
general terms ; it may be finding coarseness in 'The Circle of
the Year,' and fancy and refinement in 'Old Farmer Thomas,' and
dulness even in 'A Music Lesson.'

O FRIENDS, I thank you that you speak so plain
    By silence or by word all vaguely kind,
    And tell me that within my page you find
No word or line that with you will remain.

You help me that sweet humbleness to gain
    Which is the prize of life for human kind,
    And save from 'fiercer light' that might me blind—
Forerunner of a still more fruitless pain.

You help me still : I know from you I gain
    The fuller freedom of a muse that strives
    To mirror what is felt, and nought derives
From others, and would render joy for pain ;
    I thank you that you leave me and my lays
    To go unburdened with too grateful praise.

II.

To the many friends who told me that they had read in my book with profit and pleasure, and in some cases had got great solace and aid from it in sad moments, and the genial relief of laughter too, as life is mixed of rain and sun, of sun and rain ; and did not find 'The Circle of the Year' coarse, nor 'Old Farmer Thomas' fanciful and refined, nor 'A Music Lesson' dull or wholly without a music of its own.

O friends, how fain your praises I would turn
    To purer profit than befalls the man
    Who rests in what is done and fails to scan
Horizons wider, as his heart doth burn

Within him, nor for further flights doth yearn,
    As looking o'er his page he sees his plan
    But half-way filled : he halted as he ran :
Ah ! from your friendly words I fain would learn

A larger task, and sing more freely still
    Of joy and laughter in the sun, and take
Full hand of Nature to o'ercome the ill ;
No praise is good that doth the measure fill
    Of vanity : for life hath higher stake ;
    Your praise is sweet, but for that other's sake.

III.

Because for me I am but as a voice
   That utters what is given, or all is dark,
   Within me glows alive a little spark
Lit from a greater light, and I rejoice

   sense of my dependence : all my choice
   Is centred on my moving in that arc,
   That so I lose not radiance, and will mark
My boundaries that I fail not of my joys.

Tho' life is large, it never yet was meant
   To minister to vanity : I prize
My freedom in the light of pure intent
   To see the vision pass before mine eyes :
   If others see, it makes me long to rise,
   And if they see not, still I have my prize.

IV.

['I think there is no art which *so* reveals man to man *like*
poetry : I seem to know you, from your volume, in a way which
your prose does not open up, and which perhaps your personal
acquaintance might deny.   The function of verse, as I take it,
is to instruct, or delight, or exhort.   I find yours rich in encouragement—a quality very much *desiderated* nowadays, more
perhaps than teaching or delighting.   Your sympathies are
broad, natural and sincere, and for these I thank you.']

'Encouragement,' my 'friend,' and is it so?
　　You need it, say you, and are fain to take
　　The aid from me? the rather for my sake,
That now you know me as you wish to know.

Yes ; poetry reveals the man to man,
　　Despite the clothes, the heart that beats below ;
　　But still without 'delight' I am, and so
'Exhorting' comes within your generous plan.

Thus, then, I fall by 'exhortation' low—
　　Down to that level of your wished-for line—
A fellow full of sympathy, but no
　　'Delight' to rise to that which you incline
　　　　To honour, cherish.   'Friend,' I wish you'd say
　　　　If 'Farmer Thomas' goes the 'exhorting' way.

v.

Do my two Scotch wives, with their different views,
    Look both one way that I may thus exhort
    Through them, and yield you still the same report,
And straight myself into their life infuse?

Just read and say; if there I do not use
    The alchemy of fancy forth to pass
    From all of egotistic you could class
With your 'exhorting'?   Nay, I fain would choose

To set my men and women in your eye
    Direct and real; so you find them true
To type, and neither make to magnify
    Their virtue nor their vice; with equal due
Tell outright what in them is worst and best—
Do I in them 'exhort,' then, on your test?

VI.

A friend you had who was a friend of mine
  In olden days, and for his sake I sent
  That book to you : and all I did comment
Upon your answer was : ' No longer thine

That friend for sake of whom I did incline
  My little book unto you to present ;
  If haply it might carry some faint scent
Of olden days, and thus have welcome fine.'

To me my friend soon wrote to this effect :
  That keener irony could hardly be,
That here, as knowing, one might well detect,
  Since you and he had long ceased to agree :
Good friend, I pity you who are so small,
And could not let me pass without your gall.

VII.

How strange it is that you who surely know
    The trying joys of dialect, should *miss*
    My fine intent and highest aim in this,
Not to *exhort*, but let my good folks show

Themselves just as they are ; but here you go
    To measure me as tho' I stood for them
    Or they for me, and only to proclaim
My bounds by which you could me better know.

Is't generous or little this you call ?
    My ' friend,' you else are jealous or right small :
You either read my book and yet defy
    Its clearest claims ; or read not, and do fall
All sadly in attempt to judge.   Good-bye ;
I know you better than you fancy—I !

IV. WHY ART THOU HERE?

I.

How oft the question comes, Why art thou here,
  When others, thy superiors, pass away,
  And leave a shadow on the bright noonday,
With work half-done, and many a falling tear

Tells of the blank left in their larger sphere,
  Whilst thou art but a loiterer on the way?
  These losses on our lesser souls do lay
Fresh calls to service, and to banish fear.

They tell that we are left for purpose clear—
  To run more eager, and devote anew
Our powers to lift the burdens others bear :
Thus may we leave the saddened world more fair
  By lights of faith and hope and courage true,
Bringing the day of promised grace more near.

II.

When down the sun goes in the western sky,
  Out come the stars that fled before his light,
  Now shining as the dark grows fair and bright,
To fill with joy the weary traveller's eye,

That knows not well the path he goeth by,
  And looks above, and, to his great delight,
  One old familiar planet swims in sight,
And tells him where his wished-for goal doth lie.

So may we be as stars to those that mourn
  The loss of suns that led them on their way,
  And now might lose high heart, and long delay
Their progress onward : nay, might faint and turn
  Right backward, for the lack of guiding star
  To point them where the saints and angels are.

V. ROAMINGS.

1. AT EDZELL CASTLE.

THE shattered ornaments on wall proclaim
  Amid the wreck of years, the times of joy,
  When 'lichtsome Lindsays' could their arts employ
To harry others, and to spread their fame.

In many a rush of onset did they tame
  Their enemies ; and wassail did not cloy
  Thereafter, when they set aside annoy,
And sought their pleasure in the social flame.

The garden-bowers, clear-marked with emblems fair,
  Tell how the 'lichtsome Lindsays' aye had eye
For art and beauty ; and did nowise spare
  The spell of music : song's own witchery :
    And thus the hoary ruin tells its tale,
    With witness to a life that did not fail.

II. AT DUN HOUSE.

An ancient home, with many a record fair
   Of noble deed and generous sacrifice
   For truth and right, and all that in the eyes
Of honest Scots should be held high and rare.

An Erskine once with Knox took perilous share
   Against the league that sought even to entice
   The Scottish Lords to pawn their liberties,
And with the Papists make their praise and prayer.

In danger, exile, constant to the cause
   Of true religion, liberty and right,
   The Erskines truly walked as men of might :
To them the current of their country's laws
   Owes not a little ; and the name is bright
   With thoughts and memories shedding gracious light.

III. THE SOUTHESK.

Once more by thee, fair stream, I take my stand,
  Where, as a boy, I roved thro' summers long,
  When sunshine seemed a thousand times more strong
Than in these later summers in our land.

Oft with a youthful sportive scholar band
  Have I plied here the triple floating flies,
  And oft rewarded with the shining prize
Proudly returned, my witness in my hand.

Nought changed appears; thro' yonder leafy screen,
  A glimpse is caught of stately turret-bowers,
    Where gifted Southesk holds his ancient seat;
And yonder in the distance, poised between
  The smoky chimneys, and cathedral towers,
    Old Brechin Castle, Ramsay's proud retreat.

IV. AT PANMURE HOUSE.

The generations pass indeed, and leave
   Their records writ of mingled joy and grief :
   Well is it when there rises sweet relief
Of saintly memory telling not to grieve.

The Maules are gone ; and others hold their seat—
   Who could have guessed their vigour all so brief,
   When he that play'd such prankish jokes was lief
To go as beggar on a wager-feat ?

With children round him ; children's children too
   About his knees, as promise that the race
     Should hold its own with grace that bravery gives.
   The Maules are gone : the Ramsays hold their place,
     The lonely Lady Christian only lives
Like shining link between the old and new.

[Written September, 1881.   Lady Christian Maule, the last of
the Maules, good and benevolent, died March 21st, 1888, in her
eighty-third year.]

V. AT DUNBLANE.

How fair the lights fall on the ancient walls—
  All hoar and windowless, and marked by time,
  They tell of many a voice and prayer sublime,
That rose for Scotland at her urgent calls.

There Leighton oft to heaven upraised his hands
  In powerful pleadings for his country's weal,
  And close behind, as new the old to seal,
The later fabric all imposing stands.

And there the 'Bishop's Walk,' well sung by one
  Who teaches how the hopes of men may grow
From more to more by Mercy's benison :
  The Allan sweetly murmurs on below,
Like one, that gracious peace by love hath won ;
  And over all the mellow sunset's glow.

['The Bishop's Walk' is the first poem of mark by Dr. Walter
C. Smith, of Free High Church, Edinburgh, author of 'Olrig
Grange,' etc.]

VI. IN BISHOP LEIGHTON'S LIBRARY.

A gracious spirit cast in troublous age :
　　Not studious ease, but studious work he sought—
　　The wranglers round to fair agreement brought,
The warmest wish his spirit could engage.

When round him rose the threats of zealot rage,
　　He fain had wrapt himself in scholar's thought ;
　　But still for unity and peace he wrought
With that one weapon he could surely wage.

We read the pages that his eye oft conned,
　　The margins faintly marked with words full wise,
And reverent insight that should have atoned
　　The faults that loomed so large in bigot eyes :
　　　　A worker for the world though held in thrall,
　　　　With ready answer to each human call.

VII. WITH THE PASTOR.

How good to journey on thy rounds with thee ;
  To hear the humble wisdom of the cot,
  Unconscious evidence that thou art not
An alien, stranger, but a friend, and free

Of house and heart : no slightest joy or pain
  But finds in thee an equal answering thrill—
  True sympathizer in their good and ill :
In word and work a pastor not in vain.

Of tastes artistic, loving works of art,
  And travelled in the quest of knowledge fair,
With aptest power to illustrate the theme.
But best I love thee when thou dost not dream
  Of aught but how the losses to repair,
Of those sore pierced by fell affliction's dart.

VIII. ST. ANDREWS.

Oh, quaint cathedral city by the sea,
   How oft a vision of thy towers and fanes
   Hath risen upon me in the dingy lanes
Of London city : now I gaze on thee !

Rapt in the radiant stores thou hold'st in fee
   Of martyr-memories, 'mid thy ancient halls,
   I'd wander lonely, summoning as thralls
Or nimble friends, the fancies fair and free.

But other calls invite : dear friends I claim
   Within the ancient dual colleges
That boast their equal rights—their honoured fame
Spread wide by men of power : two late have died
   Who lit the records with their charm and grace :
And in their light our loves are multiplied.

IX. PRINCIPAL SHAIRP.

A poet in his inmost mind and heart,
   If fullest utterance on occasion failed :
   But happy that his life was ne'er assailed
By worldly ways or vanities of art.

Before his eyes he held fair Nature's chart,
   So closely rapt, that hardly did he feel
   The mighty secret strifes of men reveal,
In seeking unity of part with part.

He lived his life in Nature's company,
   His joys he found in mountain, hill, and glen ;
No solitary, yet he chose to be
   A stranger to the dubious ways of men.
     A witness for the life of thought, the good
     That comes of fair imagination's food.

X. PRINCIPAL TULLOCH.

A man of men, with happy tact and grace,
  Deep-thoughted, studious, sage in council too ;
  To all the claims of human nature true,
A patient ardour lighting up his face.

He did not arrogate his right of place,
  Yet held it in the eyes of all who knew
  His record ; and ne'er failed to render due
Wherever power or genius left its trace.

Broad as a Churchman, as a man most fair :
  Theology with him took colours new
Of life and heart ; his pen was chaste and rare,
  Directed well to beautify the true.
    Convinced of right, he never from it swerved,
    And always faithful to the Church he served.

XI. PROFESSOR JOHN VEITCH.

And one I miss hath turned him to the west,
   To hold high place as warder of the rules
   Of ordered thought, and careful test the tools
Of science' servants yet to come ; whose breast

Natheless is troubled with the sweet unrest
   Of poet's fancy, and the sense that guides
   The Nature-lover to the mountain sides—
By lonest streams to wander undistrest.

The Border and its ballads find him true
   By sympathetic tact to render back
Their misty meanings and their life renew :
   With him to pace the hard and heathery track
     Is bounteous company : the lonesome waste
     Is then by many a noble figure graced.

VI. DEDICATORY.

TO MISS MARY ANDERSON.

NATURE and Art not rivals are, but one :
    Art is forefelt in Nature, Nature yearns
    To perfect Art within her—ever turns
To see herself in mirror made of man.

And there is found the imaged perfect plan
    Of God's high purpose as true genius earns
    The mead of praise from human heart, that burns
To see the lights condensed that scattered ran.

And so I speak to preface praise, and bring
    My gift, on which thou look'st with favouring eye :
    There is a fitness in thy fame, whereby
I fain would catch the waft of sheltering wing.
    If Art may mate with Nature, simple, free,
    These two meet fair in unison in thee.

[I meant at one time to dedicate my sonnets to Miss Mary Anderson. I had even got her consent and had written the above; but she fell ill and passed out of public view, and I did not care to trouble her any further about it.]

VII. A LESSON OF CONTENTMENT.

'Be content with such things as ye have.'

I.

LATE on a winter night, returning home
From strife with worldly cares, in sombre mood,
Doubting the presence of the promised good
In evils that with later days had come;

My thoughts slipped to the brighter lot of some
Who scarce had laboured so intent, nor stood
In sun and storm, letting no aims intrude,
The thoughts enticing from one end to roam.

By gray Old Bailey, shadowed deep, and grim,
I passed, when softly on my ear there broke
Low notes of 'Jesus loves me, this I know.'
I looked, saw nought at first, and then the dim
Uncertain outlines all too clear bespoke
The child deformed that moved there, limping slow.

II.

On coming near, I said, ' My child, how glad
   Your singing makes me 'mid the cold and mist !'
   She looked surprised, as though she hardly wist
Why any should her singing so applaud.

She said, in chirping accents, nowise sad :
   ' Poor mother ails, and Sammy will insist
   On working night work, to make up the list
Of things for her : I fetch his meals, dear lad.

' I sing because it makes the way more short :
   Seems as I aye have comp'ny when I sing,
   And mother says that hymn cheers them as ail.'
O little child, how simply ye report
   Of true content, and shame me in this thing :
   This true heart's kingdom nevermore can fail.

Gentleman's Magazine.

VIII. A SUCCESSFUL EFFORT.

'A little child shall lead them.'

I saw to-day a sight that made me sigh ;
  Yet brought me soon a soothing thrill of joy :
  A little child that would, with wiles, decoy
Her tipsy father past the tempting sty

Where men seek Life in Death.   Intent her eye
  To homeward, while her little hands employ
  Themselves in his.   Delight that will not cloy!
He rises, follows, as she leads him by

The glittering doors : her thin black clothing speaks
  Of sister, brother gone, or mother lost—
  A faithful helpmate 'mid adversity.
Most like the last ; and, as the work-charged weeks
  Fly onward, may thy efforts ne'er be crost,
  To do as did thy mother good by thee.

Gentleman's Magazine.

IX. A TRICKSTER, SO.

(TO A SO-CALLED GREAT PAINTER, WHO DECLARED HIS
ART WAS TO HIM 'A MATTER MERELY OF POUNDS,
SHILLINGS, AND PENCE.')

GREAT artist are you, who can plainly say
    ' Pounds, shillings, pence' is what you make your end,
    And art mere means whereby you may ascend
To wealth and luxury?   To 'make it pay'

Is your great maxim.   Then, sir, where the play
    Of that divinest impulse keen to blend
    Inspirèd thought with touches that can bend,
As tho' upon it some Aurora lay,

The soul to soul, as flames together draw,
    Or sunflower to the sun, and leaves its trace
    Where'er 't has been, that men may look with grace
Of joy and awe forever : such a law
    Angelico lived by, and Angelo.
    But you, sir, you are but a *trickster*, so.

V. TRANSLATIONS.

I. PROEM.

To Petrarch once I gave my days
  For many a week, and heard his lute
  Breathe softly, till in me took root
The pensive thoughts that all men praise ;
And then I thought that I would raise
  A tribute to this later fruit,
  And keep my lips no longer mute,
But shape it so to soothe always.
These long have lain untouched and lone :
  I draw a few from out my store,
And give to those by whom I'm known ;
  A hurried taste, no more, no more :
    It seems a labour lost, and yet
    A few may read, and not forget.

II. SONNETS FROM PETRARCH.

I.

YE who in scattered rhymes may list the sound
   Of sighs, wherewith I daily feed my heart;
   Reviving my young error that doth part
The man I was from he that now I'm found:

Between vain hope and vainer sorrow bound,
   I would, in various style, my griefs impart;
   And hope that, if ye e'er have felt love's smart,
With pity, if not pardon, I'll be crowned.

I know full well how all men point to me,
   As one who is fit theme for talk and scorn;
   And I myself sink in my own esteem.
Of all my weakness shame the fruit must be,
   And penitence from out clear knowledge born
     That worldly pleasure is a short-lived dream.

II.

By swiftest vengeance that he might me smite,
   And punish in one day for errors vain,
   Love suddenly laid hand on bow again,
Like one who time and place hath marked aright.

My trembling heart my courage did invite
   To shield from danger what bright eyes might strain,
   When, lo ! his deadliest shaft did cleave amain
Where once fell blunted every arrow's flight.

Thus, being baffled in the first attack,
   Nor vigour left, nor space of time, had I
     To seize his arms, as I had wished to do.
Nor could I fly for shelter to the back
   Of some steep rock, where still I might defy
     The doom, that even he would scarce renew.

III.

It was the day when even the sun did pale
   His light in pity for our Maker's pain,
   That I was captured, having watched in vain,
And your sweet eyes, fair lady, did prevail.

On such a day one well might blameless fail
   To raise defence against Love's blows again ;
   Secure and unsuspecting, I walked fain :
With common sorrow thus my grief holds scale.

Love found me of my weapons all disarmed ;
   And opened thro' the eyes the heart's fair way ;
     And these since then the gate of tears have been.
Love gets no honour that he hath me harmed
   And left me wounded, piteously his prey,
     Since, being armed, he kept his bow unseen.

IV.

He Who, with infinite providence and art,
   Governs His fair creation far and near,
   Set many a star in either hemisphere
And Jove o'er Mars endowed in richer part ;

Who, when He came to earth that light to dart
   Upon Time's Scroll, and set forth, marvel-clear,
   The Eternal Truth, from fishers' humble gear
Called John and Peter to high place apart.

With His nativity He did not grace
   Great Rome, but Bethlehem ; for aye He loves
To lift the humble to the higher place !
From little hamlet shines a sun once more,
   And nature blesses it, as well behoves
Since claims it sweetest lady earth e'er bore.

V.

When moved by sighs I call thee by the name
   That in my heart is written fair of Love,
   LAUdlike it sounds, of sweetest accents wove,
As my fond tongue begins the word to frame.

Your REgal state that next asserts its claim
   Doubles my courage the emprise to prove;
   But 'Tarry' cries the last, for powers above
All that ye boast alone could reach this fame.

Thus all that call you by that word again
   Are taught at once to LAUd and to REvere,
     For praise and reverence are your rightful state:
Unless, perchance, Apollo should disdain
   The mortal tongue that, strange to fitting fear,
     Around his greeny boughs should lightly prate.

VI.

So perverse and determined is my will
  To follow her that turneth age to flee,
  And lightly from Love's chain escapeth free,
And runneth, as I slowly follow still;

And urge the more and with my utmost skill
  The safer road, the less it serveth me,
  Alike with spur and rein indifferently.
As Love, perverse by nature, works me ill:

And then the reins he gathers up by force,
  And I to him am subject most complete,
    Who drives me, thus unwilling, to my death,
And all to reach the laurel, now the source
  Of bitter fruit that adds but feverish heat
    To former pains, and no way comforteth.

VII.

Intemperance, slumber and the slothful down
   Have banished virtue from this world of ours;
   Our nature wanders from the course—great powers
Hath custom to pluck off our manhood's crown.

Quenched thus each heavenly light we ought to own
   As sent by heaven to fashion human flowers,
   And he whom Helicon with favour dowers
A thing of scorn is deemed by all the town.

Who would the laurel or the myrtle wear?
   ' Philosophy, ye poor and naked go !'
     Cry all the crowd intent on vulgar prize;
'Few comrades ye shall have as on ye fare.'
   The more I pray you, gentle spirit, show
     Thy faith in my magnanimous emprise.

VIII.

Beneath the hills where first the beauteous vest
   Of earthly members took that lady fair,
   Who oft from sleep awakes with tearful care
Him that hath sent us to her fitly drest ;

There passed we freely, by no fears opprest,
   Loving our life so sweet to creature's share,
   Without suspicion winged our flight thro' air,
By mazy ways and nothing could molest.

But in this lowly state that now we see,
   Downfallen from that other life serene,
     One only comfort from our death we gain :
That vengeance follows him that made decree
   Against us thus, bound fast as he has been,
     And as Time rolls by ever heavier chain.

IX.

When comes the planet marking out the hours,
   To take abode with Taurus once again,
   Then virtue from the flaming horn doth rain
New colours on the world in gracious showers;

Nor decks outside alone : the banks with flowers
   And hills with blossoms to the sight most fain;
   But inward where no sunrays entrance gain,
The moist earth owns its fruitful quickening powers.

Whence come these fruits and others like them too :
   So likewise she amidst our ladies Sun
     Moves life in me when light falls from her eyes.
Come thoughts of love, good acts and words not few;
   For, as she turns and bids, I, willing, run,
     But Spring ne'er visits me with sweet surprise.

x.

Colonna glorious, like a column strong,
   Our hopes thou bearest of the Latin name,
   Thou still dost calmly hold thy virtuous fame
Even while the Pope condemns thee as for wrong.

Here is no palace, theatre, galleries long,
   But fir, and beech, and pine put forth their claim
   To stir the soul with true poetic flame
Amid green grass, and hills, and sweet birds' song.

Raised from the earth to heaven our spirits soar,
   While soft the nightingale in woodland shade
      Pours all night long his melancholy strain.
With loving thoughts the heart grows more and more;
   Oh, why is scene so fair imperfect made
      Because my lord must absent still remain ?

XVI.

When all my thoughts I turn to that one part
   Where face of Laura fair I see in light,
   And burns within my mind that beauteous light—
That then consumes me inward every part.

Ah, then, I dread it from my heart should part,
   And quenched should be my perilous, sweet light—
   To go on groping blindly for that light,
Like one that knows not how to go, nor part.

So flee I from the blow which is as death,
   Though not so swiftly but I still desire
     That I should not without it fare alone.
Silent I go ; though these my words, like death,
   Would melt all hearts ; yet only I desire
     Such sighs and tears should fall from me alone.

LXXIII.

When thro' my eyes into my heart's profound
   You send your noble image, all else goes ;
   And all the powers that in my soul do close
Lapse, and my limbs like moveless weights are bound.

And from that marvel springs another ground
   Of marvel, for the chased-out part that flows
   Or fast flies from itself, thwarted, bestows
On exile easing, with revenge's bound.

Two faces hence put on one deadly hue
   For lively vigour that erst did them grace,
   And neither here nor elsewhere holds its place.
And this remembered I in piteous case
   When I beheld two lovers how they grew
   Just as my face then was to gazer's view.

CCXXVI.

(Penultimate sonnet to Laura in Life.)

In hope is his only support in wretchedness.

Heart hard and cold, and cruellest will, that lie
  In angel form, so sweet and gentle fair ;
  If for long time such rigours she prepare,
Small honour waits her in her victory.

When herbs and flowers spring up, or when they die,
  When night grows dark, or day brings softer air,
  I weep alway ; for Fortune's load I bear :
From love and Laura cause of grief have I.

In hope I live alone : remembering aye
  How by the fall of droplets steadily
    Marble I've seen consumed, and hardest stone.
Surely the coldest heart will then give way
  To tears and prayers that constant fall from me,
    And grow to warmth, and all my fervour own.

III. THE SONG OF THE BUTTERFLY.*

(FROM HERDER.)

LOVELY, light, as cloud in sky,
    Butterfly,
Over flowers thou flittest free,
Dew and blossom food for thee ;
Thyself a blossom, flying leaf ;
Who purpled thee by rosy finger's
    Touch so brief?

Was it a sylph, that thy sweet dress
    Did so impress ?
Of morning odours moulded fine
Thy beauty for one day to shine ?
O little soul, and thy small heart
Beats quickly 'neath my finger there,
    And feels death's smart.

Fly hence, O littie soul, and be
    Bright and free ;
To me an image of that birth
When man, the chrysalis of earth,
Like thee, a Zephyr shall become,
And kiss in odour, dew, and honey,
    Every bloom.

* See Opinions on ' Circle of the Year' : Mr. Joseph Skipsey.

IV. FATE.

(FROM HERDER.)

Thy fate, oh, call not cruel only,
Name not envy as its end ;
Eternal truth its law had stood,
The purity of God its good,
Necessity its might to blend.

V. FIR-TREE AND PALM.

(FROM HEINE.)

A fir-tree stands all lonely
  In the north, on a cold gray height ;
He slumbers, as round him ice and snow
  Weave a mantle of spotless white.

He dreams of a palm-tree towering
  Afar in the Eastern land,
Alone, and silently dreaming
  'Mid rocks and burning sand.

From MRS. AUGUSTA WEBSTER, March 9, 1893.

'Several of the sonnets have much interested me, and I very certainly do not agree with your friend, A. N. of the "Envoi," who dissuaded you from "the bold emprise." One of the descriptive sonnets I like is one that has a memory of spring in the autumn—the one with a squirrel in it.'

From HALL CAINE, ESQ., January 10, 1893.

'I had no idea that you were so far afield with the muses, that you were an expert at the sonnet, and had tried your wings at a flight like "The Northern Farmer." Old Thomas's story is quite admirable—vivid, racy, and true—the little closing hint of indecorums not being the least of the old man's charms.'

From THE HON. RODEN NOEL, January 30, 1893.

'Some of the sonnets have much beauty, and have given me pleasure in reading them, though perhaps the humorous poems in dialect are the most remarkable—they are really very good. But I see tender, loving observation which gives real poetical beauty to many of the pieces in their descriptions of nature, their elevation of thought, and in the reflective passages.'

From AUSTIN DOBSON, ESQ., October 26, 1874.

' I have just been reading your poem ["A Music Lesson"] to my wife, and we admire it much.   This stanza—

> It's nae alane by blawin' strang
> But eke by blawin' true
> That ye can mak' the music
> To thrill folk thro' and thro',—

may stand for poets as well as other pipers. If I may single out another verse (without any violence to the whole), I greatly like the last but one.'

April 26, 1876.

' I must tell you how *much* I like " In the Snowdrift." How simply good and pathetic, and how effective the refrain ! It is an honour to me to appear in the same number, though it is a disadvantage as well, since the comparison shows how very vital is modern humanity compared with dead classicism.'

May 9, 1876.

' I hope you got my note about the piper, which I like as much as ever.'

November 8, 1892.

' I am much gratified by your kind sonnet ; thank you very much for it. I have been reading the others with much pleasure. The " Swinburne " seems to me especially good.   In this " scanty plot of ground " you work with a dexterity that is all the more wonderful to me, because a sonnet *to my mind* is the most stubborn of forms.'

From W. M. ROSSETTI, ESQ., January 18, 1893.

' I at once looked at the sonnet on my brother, and read it with great pleasure.   It is a fine tribute to the *esoteric sense* so constantly present in his works.'

From JOHN H. INGRAM, *ESQ., Author of the 'Life of Poe,'
etc., February* 22, 1893.

'For the life of me can I understand why you do not publish. Why, "Old Farmer Thomas" alone would make a reputation. He is a worthy companion for Tennyson's "Northern Farmer." His sly pawkie humour, snatches of worldly wisdom, and longing for the past times—"good old times"—and determination to *forget the future*, are magnificent. And he is so true, so typical —that I am sure you will have people recognising him in every county, and, indeed, in various countries. I do hope whoever writes the article on Dr. Japp in Miles's poets will give that as a specimen of his powers. "Oh, my auld gudeman" and its companion piece are both also excellent samples of their author's different methods. "Sister Helen" is a poem that, in a different way, strikes home. *Do* publish : a friend—not a literary man— who has just been reading "Farmer Thomas," says, "Why does Dr. Japp not publish? Why, this is wonderful—just like what I've heard in the country."'

From J. ASHCROFT NOBLE, *ESQ., January* 11, 1893.

'The shrewd, humorous "Farmer Thomas" is in every way excellent, but I think I like the nature sonnets as much as anything. What seems to me to be essential in a nature poem is that it should carry with it the very feeling of the scene or season which it celebrates, and this is what your poems do. . . . All the memorial sonnets seem to me very beautiful and tender, both those in which the loss mourned is that of some friend of yourself or of the world, and those—such as "In Memoriam," "E. F. J." and "What remains?" which express the pang of a more personal and poignant grief. In the freemasonry of sorrow, only the brotherhood can interpret the sign which tells of initiation, and I do not wonder that these poems have *found* many who have suffered, as they find me.'

From GEORGE STRONACH, ESQ., *Advocate's Library,*
Edinburgh.

' I thank you heartily for your charming volume. . . . I am well acquainted with your work, and have many a time thoroughly enjoyed it. Your "Little Baby" is an especial favourite of mine, and in reviewing Mr. Eric Robertson's collection for the *Pall Mall* I pointed out its omission.'

From ALEXANDER TAYLOR INNES, ESQ., *Advocate,*
January 5, 1893.

' I find myself so much interested in getting through your book, not only as a reader or critic, but, if I may say so, getting entangled in the personal and autobiographical interests, that I can no longer delay to thank you. Some of your sonnets have gone home very close to my heart and experience, as they will, I think, to all who have lost faces which the returning years do not restore, and long before this book comes out to take its place in the open (as it no doubt will), you will find that it has prepossessed and purchased a place in the affections of those to whom you have been good enough to send it. With very many thanks, and all good wishes for the years to come, for you and for the harp which sighs to our north-wind even by the waters of Babylon.'

From MACKENZIE BELL, ESQ., *December* 31, 1892.

' Honestly, I think this book ought to give you a place among the poets of our time.'

From J. R. FINDLAY, ESQ., *January* 4, 1893.

' You have a genuine command of the sonnet ; the difficulty of the generalship there I know, for I have tried the same ! But where did you get that delightfully lightsome form thereof which you use in the Parisian quartette? "Old Farmer Thomas" is admirable : it recalls the "Northern Farmer," of course, but is distinct and individual. The last verses are particularly good.'

*From CHARLES H. SMITH, ESQ., of Redbury, Ardleigh,
Essex, January 5, 1893.*

'I think "Farmer Thomas's Tale" is in its own line one of
the most delightful things I have read. My wife and her sisters
have been taking advantage of my absence, and been reading
the volume to one another, and, although they know it is pre-
sumption on their part to express an opinion, they think in not
publishing you are depriving the world of a very great deal of
pleasure.'

*From MRS. BROTHERTON, The Elms, Freshwater,
January 5, 1893.*

'I think there is great beauty in much of the Seasons poem
(for it is *one* poem, though many). But the dialect poems made
me laugh (in spite of my neuralgia), and I think "Farmer
Thomas's Tale" is capital. But I believe I really enjoyed the
last poem in the book quite specially—"The Music Lesson."
It is admirable, and a friend coming in while I was still enjoying
it, I could not help speaking of it, and even reading it to her,
and she was delighted with its humour and racy pathos (if I may
couple the epithets).'

January 16, 1893.

'Many of the sonnets I specially care for, and I find some of
the lyrics full of tenderness and grace. "Brave Brother Ned"
is a touching little poem, for instance.'

January 21, 1893.

'He [Lord Tennyson] spoke of your volume, as having found
much pleasure in it, as I dare say he told you. He liked very
much the sonnets to his father, which he thought full of feeling
and grace. And he quite agreed with me in my admiration for
"The Music Lesson," which really is a gem of the first water.'

From MACKENZIE BELL, ESQ., January 10, 1893.

'The other day Mr. Theodore Watts talked to me about your poems. He likes them not a little, and it seems that Mr. Swinburne thinks your sonnet on himself very fine.'

From JAMES T. BLACK, ESQ., of Messrs. Adam and Charles Black, January 20, 1893.

'The volume came to me at a rather sad time, which is one reason for my being so tardy in acknowledging it, but I found in it many poems full of human sympathy, and well suited to afford solace at a time of affliction. I cannot pretend to be a great judge of poetry, but I admire very much the various pieces in your volume.'

From MR. JOSEPH SKIPSEY, January 6, 1893.

'I was not prepared to find you the author of so many lovely poems as I meet with in this book. I am touched, and especially with regard to those in the sonnet form—with the subtlety of thought, the tenderness, the pathos, and the grace, the simplicity and naturalness of expression, and the flute-like melody that characterizes them.'

March 10, 1893.

'Many of your poems I have read again and again, and each time with increase of joy. They are natural, tender, sweet and musical. "Echoes," "The Unseen Singer," "The Dance of the Flowers," "Sultan Soliman and the Birds," "Fairy Music," are all fine, and especially so is "Dawn in the Swiss Mountains." Again, as a piece of blank verse I know nothing more charming than "White Campion." This, again, is a gem without a flaw. Your translation of Goethe's "Flower Girls" is inimitable. But why, my dear Dr. Japp, have you not included your translation of Herder's "Butterfly," which is so felicitous I never could forget it? "The Flower Girls" and "The Butterfly" would have proved you a poet, had you written nothing else ; but surely the charming " Flower Girls " ought to have been attended by the beautiful " Butterfly."*

From JOHN MALCOLM BULLOCH, *ESQ., M.A., of the* '*Sketch*,' *March* 13, 1893.

'The dialect story ["Farmer Thomas"] is inimitable. I like the vivid contrast in the old man between his wisdom as gained from a life's experience, and his repudiation of all wisdom acquired by educative processes which he has been denied. You have unquestionably caught the spirit of the sonnet. One of the best I think is that on "Hop-picking," where the contrast between the freedom of nature and the bondage of mammon is brought finely out. The ballads, like the One-and-twenty song, are charming, and the variety of mood and metre is very enlivening. I keep your book on my writing-table, so that at odd times I may escape from this desert of yellow brick for a breeze at Cowie or the hedge of a Kentish lane.'

From MRS. BAIRD SMITH, *January* 19, 1893.

' I mark as I go on those I specially delight in, and I am finding those most marked are the sonnets of *personal* reminiscence, and still more the sonnets of pure nature. These latter, so far as I have gone, seem to me gems, like the exquisite bit of prose you wrote in the *Argosy* about your vicar's garden. So far is enough, may be, for one who is neither a critic nor the son of a critic, thanks be to God, for I enjoy all the more.'

April 7, 1893.

' I have wanted to tell you that I continue to find great pleasure in your poems. I still cling to your nature poems. It is so rare for the "words, words" of dealers with nature to rouse any feeling in me save that of irritation, that I can not help thinking your poems, which not only bring a picture to the

---

* Mr. Skipsey recalled to my mind thus a whole series of translations from the German I had quite forgotten. The ' Butterfly' is given in this volume.

mind's eye, but bring back all the glorious and lovely associations of glorious and lovely scenery itself, must possess a rare power —at any rate, to me they do.'

From MISS DE QUINCEY, Hyères, January 18, 1893.

' I have been reading your poems with much pleasure, and have found many favourites, many beauties. The sonnet to " Campbell of Row," and the one above it about " Row and Roseneath," I think especially beautiful. Then, " The Tangled Skein " and " Sister Helen " are, in another way, very fine. The " Tangled Skein " has so much truth in it—deeper truths than appear on the surface. All those treating of Scotch scenery strike one much here.'

From MRS. ISABELLA FYVIE MAYO (Edward Garrett), January 24, 1893.

' I think " Farmer Thomas " is a fine old heathen finely pictured—a survival of primitive man among Christianity and civilization. *I have met " Farmer Thomas."* My own delight is especially in " The Circle of the Year " *sonnets.* Some of them I read over and over again, with the feeling that I know their scenery and their symbols, and they always make me home-sick for the sweet scenery of Southern England.'

From MRS. WESTWOOD, widow of Thomas Westwood, Author of ' The Sangreal,' etc., January 21, 1893.

' Your book was a delightful Christmas present. I have now read the poems with great interest. I like them much ; they are full of thought and of the true sentiment of their various subjects ; they will, I am sure, be very successful, and I think you are too modest in refusing them a chance with the public. " Old Farmer Thomas " is very clever and amusing. I read it aloud a night or two ago to friends who enjoyed it. The " Touch and Go " poems are charming for children, old and young, truly.'

From ERIC MACKAY, ESQ., Author of 'Songs of a Violinist,' etc.

'Your book is full of beautiful things, and I thank you heartily for it. What a pity you restrict it to private circulation !'

From CHARLES POLLITT, ESQ., of 'Westmorland Gazette.'

'On reaching home from London on Wednesday night, I found your welcome volume of poems. Tired as 250 miles' jolting had made me, I couldn't help dipping into the tempting little volume, and once begun, I found myself absorbed up till bedtime. I could not help *stealing* your fine sonnet on Wordsworth and giving it in the *Gazette* this week.' (Mr. Pollitt, in the *Gazette*, also spoke in the highest terms of the sonnets, with reminiscences of early days.)

From the REV. WILLIAM HASTIE, M.A., B.D., Examiner in Theology, University of Edinburgh.

'I have been enjoying in considerable detail your fine poetic fancies and music during these days. Thank you most heartily for your charming and interesting little volume, which is full of poetic life in finely developed power, and extraordinary variety and ease of movement. I found a special message in Sonnet xxi., p. 29, "Lose not Hope"; and living sympathy with you everywhere. And you are everywhere—all round, and in the "circle" not only "of the year," but of life itself. I mean to return again and again to your muse for new thought and comfort.'

From EDMUND CLARENCE STEDMAN, ESQ., New York, January 28, 1893.

'I have already read enough, chiefly among your sonnets, to assure me that I shall wish to read more. I note the modest personal note at the outset; it at once draws to you the affection of a recipient of a copy of this select edition. If I live to make a final revision of the V. P. [Victorian Poets], I hope to pay some tribute to you. . . . [Later, March 27.] I think that

Watts, Swinburne, Morris, and Dobson may well be charmed to be placed in your cycle, and saluted, not by the "awkward squad," which poor Burns so feared, but in verse which does them and you equal honour.'

From MRS. ISA CRAIG KNOX, January 30, 1893.

'I have read your volume with the greatest pleasure, and do not mean to lay it aside. It is an added pleasure to have a gift with such associations. . . . I have now made for myself a life of domestic and neighbourly duty, which might be described in some of the lines of your beautiful Sonnet xvi.'

From the REV. DR. DONALD MACLEOD, April 26, 1893.

'I have taken the sonnets on "Sorrow" by themselves, and feel their pathos and truth ; but I must confess I like the rum old "Farmer Thomas" best of all—racy, sharply characterized, and deliciously original. I chuckled over each fresh revelation.'

*From CHARLES W. WOOD, ESQ., Editor of the 'Argosy,'
February* 2, 1893.

'I had no idea, until I saw your verses in this form, that you had so largely and truly the gift of poetry. I had no idea that you had written so much, and much as I have liked your prose, and felt and appreciated your powers of mind, I did not know that poetry was so distinctly amongst them. I think your "Dream" from Tel-el-Amarna is very charming, and agree with Professor Flinders Petrie, that you have entered into the very spirit of the scene and incident. But, then, I think the book is full of gems. I was delighted to have it, the more that it cannot be bought.'

*From MISS J. E. A. BROWN, Author of 'Lights through a
Lattice,' etc., January* 3, 1893.

'I have to thank you very much for remembering me amongst your "friends," and for sending me your beautiful book. . . . Opening the pages here and there, I find some lovely lines which will dwell with me, such as—to take almost at haphazard—page 81 :

> " The darkening eve is dawn to other skies :
> All ends are but beginnings otherwhere :
> New dawns from darkness that all life renew."

I like these lines very much.   Again, " Swallows " :

> " O wingèd memories of the blissful days
> When cares lay light as dew upon the leaves."

Thank you very much for your book.'

From PROFESSOR S. S. LAURIE, Edinburgh, February 21, 1893.

' I have read your book with the very greatest of pleasure. " Dawn in the Swiss Mountains," " Farmer Thomas's Tale," and the sonnet on Austin Dobson, are all of a very different character ; but all, indeed, have impressed me in a very marked way. They are distinctly successful expressions of poetic faculty. . . . The amount of genuine thought in your pieces is a protest against the mere glare of radiant phraseology which characterizes a school too popular.'

From the REV. DR. GEORGE JOHNSTON, Liverpool, Ex-Moderator of the Presbyterian Church of England, December 30, 1893.

' My wife read to me " Old Farmer Thomas's Tale," and we enjoyed it very much.   How this piece first turned up I know not, but it did, and we had a good twenty minutes' quiet pleasure out of it.'

From DANIEL RICKETSON, ESQ., New Bedford, Mass., January 30, 1893.

' I have read a goodly number of the poems, and my wife has read to me, from time to time, a good many more.   They are the product of a true poetic talent and a scholarly mind.   Among the poems, I particularly noted the one " In Memoriam E. F. J." *What comes from the heart goes to the heart.'*

From SIR GEORGE REID, *P.R.S.A., January* 6, 1893.

' I have not yet had time to read all the volume ; but I soon lighted on the sonnets on Chalmers and on Sir W. Fettes Douglas, which are to my mind admirable, especially the latter —so very true to the place and its associations.'

From PROFESSOR W. F. BARRETT, *Dublin, January* 9, 1893.

' Thank you a thousand times for so charming a memorial of yourself and of your many-sided and gifted literary life.   Already I have read aloud some of your sonnets and shorter poems, and my sisters are urging me to go on.   But why did you not publish the volume ? So many, I am sure, would like to have procured a copy.   However, it has a greater value as it is to the fortunate friends to whom you have sent it.'

From the REV. DR. JAMES ROBERTSON, *Professor of Oriental Languages, Glasgow, January* 6, 1893.

' It is just the kind of book I like to have beside me to take up now and then.   I value it most, however, for the fact that you include me in the circle of friends to whom you seek to give pleasure.   You have done well to gather these poems together, and you have no reason to be ashamed of anything in this volume.   I understand quite well what you mean by deprecating notices and criticisms.   But you will not object to the criticism of one of your friends, who, judging simply by what he likes, declares the volume a great treat.'

From MISS AGNES REPPLIER, *Philadelphia, U.S.A., March* 27, 1893.

' " Farmer Thomas " pleased me best—pleased me very much indeed, and so did the light-hearted, fanciful verses for children. . . . I most sincerely thank you for the kind-hearted whim that moved you to send such a boon to a stranger beyond the sea.'

From the late revered PROFESSOR E. L. LUSHINGTON,
January 24, 1893.

'You will, I fear, have thought me unwarrantably tardy in not sooner thanking you for your kind gift ; but perhaps you will, to some extent, excuse me when you learn that, for several weeks, I have been a patient in the doctor's hands, confined to my room and to bed for all but an hour or two of the day, and the weakness attendant upon this condition indisposes one much for any exertion. I have read much of your volume with great pleasure and interest ; the feeling is always healthy and good, combined often with freshness, lucidity and grace ; the sonnet of dedication touched me much, and many other pieces.'

[Had I known Mr. Lushington was so ill, I should never have troubled him with the book, and yet, maybe, it relieved a weary hour or two for him in the illness from which he never recovered.]

From MRS. MINTO, *dated Aberdeen, January* 6, 1893.

'My husband has been confined to bed for some days with a severe bronchial cold, and unable for correspondence, otherwise he would sooner have acknowledged your kind New Year's gift of verse. He bids me say how pleased he was to receive it. He has dipped into it here and there, and found it full of interest, and beauty, and marked personality ; and he anticipates much pleasure in reading it at length.'

'It is, perhaps, hardly right to include in this notice Dr. A. H. Japp's " Circle of the Year," etc. But many of the poems have appeared in periodicals, and it may be hoped that before very long Dr. Japp will see the wisdom of making this volume more readily accessible. . . . Among the sonnets, especially, are many fine and beautiful things, such as the series on " Great Poets," from which we may cite the following on Tennyson. . . .'—MR. JAMES BRITTEN, F.L.S., in ' Nature Notes.'

*From E. H. K. at Montclar, Aouste, Drôme, France,
January 3, 1893.*

'At last I have " The Unseen Singers," for which I have waited
full five years. Your book would give pleasure to many more
than your friends, I think ; but to one of your friends at least
it has given pleasure of the intensest kind. It will always be one
of my most cherished book companions, and go with me everywhere. I have not had a spark of poetry in me since I came to
France, but it caught fire last night, and I send you my thanks
in rhyme ; the two sonnets have at least the merit of expressing
most truly my feelings.

'TO DR. A. H. JAPP.

'ON RECEIVING " THE CIRCLE OF THE YEAR."

I.

'Oh, Friend, I hold thy book with reverent hand,
  The leaves fresh cut, my dim eyes seeing there
  Old scenes and faces fair—ah, wondrous fair !
A dear, lost home, sweet word ! In foreign land
My heart has learned how sweet. Again I stand
  By northern seas, blue spaced ; again I share
  With lovely souls now gone, thoughts high and rare
From treasuries of poets, full and grand.
So, reading here and there, the page I turned,
  And, set to music sweet, dear names I found,
  Of those beloved of old. On holy ground
  I seemed to stand, amid the saints in light,
  Who wait for us, still in the earthly fight ;
And as I read, my heart within me burned.

II.

' Oh, magic spell of ordered words that wake
  Long-sleeping memories of forgotten years,
  Half seen at first through mist of veiling tears,
Till through the gloom familiar forms they take,

And echoes of long-silent voices break
  Upon the air. Lo ! now the vision clears
  As some fair landscape when the dawn appears,
And sight and sound one joy harmonious make.
So comes the past upon me, as I look
  Upon these pages, richer far to me
  With buried treasure, than the boundless sea
  To him who seeks its pearls. These coldly shine ;
  Those ever sparkle with a light divine.
So, from my heart, I thank thee for thy book.

'E. H. K.'

THE END.

BILLING AND SONS, PRINTERS, GUILDFORD.

www.ingramcontent.com/pod-product-compliance
Lightning Source LLC
Chambersburg PA
CBHW021120020726
47500CB00003B/852